A *Worthy* Heir

Pat Ballard

Pearlsong Press
Nashville, TN

Pearlsong Press
P.O. Box 58065
Nashville, TN 37205
www.pearlsong.com

ISBN: 0-9713247-8-6
Library of Congress Control Number: 2004104469

This book contains the text of the 2003 softcover edition published
by Writers Club Press, an imprint of iUniverse.com, as well as
additional material.

Other books by Pat Ballard available from Pearlsong Press:

Dangerous Curves Ahead: Short Stories
His Brother's Child
Nobody's Perfect
Wanted: One Groom

In memory of my mother,
who taught me that true beauty comes from within.

Chapter 1

Pam Spencer's eyes flew quickly back to the message in the Public Notice section of the morning paper.

> *Local business tycoon Fiona Bainbridge has disowned her only heir, and seeks a worthy heir to inherit her millions. If you think you might qualify, call Bainbridge Corporation for details.*

Without taking time to think about it, for fear she'd change her mind, Pam picked up the phone and dialed the number she hastily looked up in the Yellow Pages of the phone book.

The next morning found Pam sitting in a huge conference room at an oversized oval table, staring at an application that resembled a combination of a job application and a health insurance application.

Glancing around the room at several other people filling out the same kind of forms, Pam felt the old bitterness rising up inside her again. *Nobody here deserves this more than Tom and me,* she thought.

At the end of the application was a request for a brief essay on why the applicant felt they were worthy to become the Bainbridge heir. Pamela had no problem writing an impressive essay to answer that question.

She felt the beginning of a tension headache as she turned the key in the door of the small two-bedroom apartment she and Tom shared.

She felt it quickly magnify as she became aware of Tom, sitting in his wheelchair at their small dinette table, holding the newspaper. Drat! She'd meant to throw the Public Notice section away before she left this morning.

"Pamela Spencer, what *is* this?"

"What's what?" she innocently asked, as she tossed her purse onto the table and headed for the medicine cabinet to get something for her headache.

"Don't even for one minute try to act like you don't know why this notice about Bainbridge Corporation is circled in red, with the telephone number written beside it. I might be crippled, but I'm not crazy. Not yet."

Pamela ran water into a glass and swallowed the pills, stalling for a little time before answering him.

"Pam?"

"I'm coming, Tom," she reluctantly responded, pulling out a chair and sitting down at the table across from him.

"Now, what do you want to know?"

"I want to know what crazy stunt you've pulled," he answered through clenched teeth.

Tom hadn't been the same since his accident. His once happy-go-lucky nature had disappeared and been replaced by a sour, bitter disposition. Tom, her beloved older brother, who had always looked after and taken care of her, had become dependent on her instead, and it was slowly destroying him.

"Tom, please listen to me before you jump to conclusions," she pleaded. "Don't you understand what this could do for us? It could give us back all we've lost. It could give you that back surgery you so desperately need."

"Do you honestly believe a company that I filed a lawsuit against would consider making you an heir to the owner's millions of dollars? Pam, get real. They'll laugh in your face."

"Maybe they won't find out that you tried to sue them and lost." Pam was an incurable optimist, even in the face of the most desperate times. She always felt there was a pot of gold at the end of the rainbow.

"Pam, you're dreaming again. Give it up. Accept the fact that I'm stuck in this chair for life. Stop trying to fix my life and get on with yours. You're too young to be burdened down with trying to take care of me. Trust me, I *can* exist without you."

Pam met Tom's stubborn stare eye to eye. He might have lost his happy-go-lucky nature, but he still had the Spencer stubbornness. Well, she had a good case of the same stubbornness, and she wasn't about to give up on him.

"We've had this discussion enough in the past that you should know by now I'm not listening. You can't give up, Tom. We've got to find a way to win this battle. The doctors say you can walk again if you could only get the surgery."

"Yeah, that's what they say. But not a one of them has offered to pay for it out of their own pocket, have they? They won't touch me without insurance, and how many insurance companies have we called? A hundred? More? None of them will touch me because Bainbridge Corporation insurance dropped me, and I have a pre-existing condition. And yet, you preach to me about not giving up. Pam, you live in a world of denial, but I live in the real world of facts. The fact of this damn chair I've been sentenced to for life."

"But, Tom—"

"No! I'm weary of this discussion. Now, once again, what did you do this morning?"

"I went down to Bainbridge Corporation and put in an application to become heir to the inheritance." Pam's chin went up in defiance as she glared at Tom.

"Well, you can call them and tell them that you withdraw your application." Tom glared back at her.

It had been a long time since they'd argued about anything. They'd never argued much, since Tom was seven years older than Pam and had always been her "protector," especially after losing both their parents within a year of each other from terminal illnesses. But occasionally they did disagree, and when they did, it was usually a strong confrontation.

Pam's headache was getting worse, and she didn't feel like arguing anymore, so she said, "Okay, Tom, I'll call them later today and tell them to withdraw my application." She hoped the resignation in her voice sounded sincere, so he'd believe her and drop the subject. In actuality, she had no intention of calling and withdrawing the application.

"That's a good girl," Tom said. He wheeled his chair to the section of the apartment that was designated as the living room and clicked on the TV.

Pam watched sadly as he found one of the programs he watched each day, just trying to keep his mind off the constant pain he was in, both mentally and physically. She knew the pain he suffered from his back injury must be horrible, because she saw him grimace sometimes when he didn't think she was watching. And the frown lines between his eyes were deepening each day.

Since the insurance company had dropped him they couldn't afford the proper prescription drugs that would help alleviate the pain, so all he took for his constant hurting was over-the-counter medicine, which barely helped at all.

Damn the insurance companies! And damn the money-hungry doctors who wouldn't help him because he didn't have insurance!

And since all their problems had started the day Tom got hurt on the job at Bainbridge Corporation, justice would surely be done if the Bainbridge money helped him get well.

Feeling justified in her decision to pursue the Bainbridge money, and to even deceive Tom into believing she would withdraw the application, she proceeded to get ready to go to one of the two jobs she worked at just to keep their heads above the financial waters that kept threatening to drown them.

A few days later, as Pam worked busily at her main job as office manager of a small law firm, the phone rang.

"Winger & Thomas," she answered, "this is Pam."

"Pamela Spencer, please."

"This is she."

"Miss Spencer, this is Sharon Anderson, Fiona Bainbridge's executive assistant. Ms. Bainbridge wants to meet with you at ten o'clock tomorrow morning. Can you be here?" The voice sounded cold and disapproving.

"Yes, I can be there." Pam's pounding heart almost drowned out her voice. "Where do I go for the meeting?"

"Just come to the main office of Bainbridge Corporation, and we'll direct you from there."

Before Pam could agree, the phone went dead. *What's stuck in her craw?* she wondered, staring briefly at the receiver in her hand.

Sharon Anderson was as cold and disapproving in person as she'd seemed on the phone, Pam decided as she sat in the plush office of Bainbridge Corporation and waited to be called in for her interview with Fiona Bainbridge.

Sharon's platinum blonde hair seemed totally out of place against her dark complexion and almost black eyes. Eyes that held contempt when they rested briefly on Pam.

"This way," Sharon directed, leading led Pam down a long hallway.

Even with her pounding heart and sweaty palms Pam couldn't help but be amused at the tight-fitting dress that clung to and tried to ride up Sharon's slim hips as she led the way. *Why do women wear clothes they have to fight with all day?* she mused.

Sharon knocked briefly on the door before she opened it to expose a large, luxurious office, with a desk in front of windows that looked out over the Dallas skyline.

"Miss Spencer is here, Ms Bainbridge," Sharon announced to the back of a tall leather chair that was facing the window. Even though Pam was aware of the slight hint of disdain on her name, Sharon's voice was noticeably softer when she spoke to the person in the chair.

"Thank you, Sharon," a strong female voice answered. "You may go now."

With a barely audible sound of contempt, Sharon closed the door behind her.

Slowly the tall chair turned to face Pam, who was still standing in the middle of the room.

She had wondered what the mysterious Fiona Bainbridge would look like, but she would never have expected the small, frail figure that faced her. Especially after hearing the strong voice first. The piercing blue eyes that seemed to flash little rays of light as they perused Pam looked out of place on the withered face.

After what seemed to Pam like an eternity, a wide smile broke across the thin face, reminding her of sunshine bursting out from behind a severe thundercloud.

"Perfect!" Fiona declared. "I like what I see. Now if I like what's inside your head as much as how your outside looks, we may have something going on here. Come. Have a seat." And she pointed to a plush, upholstered chair that was opposite her desk.

Pam sat down, mesmerized by the person in front of her. The eyes and voice seemed to belong to a different person than the tiny frame in front of her. She fought the urge to search the room for a hidden projector that was hologramming the image she was seeing.

"Relax. I just want to ask you a few questions. This shouldn't take long. My staff has done a very good background check on you, and I have it right here in your file."

And that's supposed to make me feel better? Pam wondered.

"What makes you think you're a worthy heir to inherit my money that I've worked so hard for?" The question was shot at Pam with no warning.

"I don't think I'm worthy. There's no way I could be deserving of your money, but I need it, and that's why I answered your ad." Pam had never been one to mince words when stating her point of view.

"Very good answer. But why do you need my money?"

"I have a brother who's in desperate need of back surgery. He lost his job, and his insurance, and can't get new insurance, so we can't afford the surgery."

"So you're asking for the money for your brother and don't care anything about it for yourself?"

"That's correct."

"So you're trying to tell me you haven't had any daydreams about buying fancy cars and clothes and maybe a new house with my money? My report says you live in a small two-bedroom apartment in a complex that's not exactly in the best neighborhood." Pam felt pierced to the soul as those blue eyes penned her to her chair.

"No. I've only thought about the money for my brother's back surgery. I've never had those things you mentioned before, and I'm sure I can live the rest of my life without them."

"But they would be nice, wouldn't they?"

"A gold-plated commode would be nice, but I don't daydream about having one," Pam answered, knowing she was being disrespectful. She'd known this wasn't going to be easy, and that she'd have to swallow a lot of pride. *Remember, you're doing this for Tom*, she chided herself. *Keep your cool.* She expected anything but the cackling laugh that burst from the woman.

"Spunk! That's good. Would that brother happen to be Tom Spencer?"

Here it was. The question Pam had been dreading the most.

"Yes."

"So, you, Pam Spencer, think you can come in here and try to get my millions for your brother, who tried to sue my company?"

"Mrs. Bainbridge, your staff seems to have done a good job in checking my background. Surely, you have the facts before you as to why Tom tried to sue Bainbridge Corporation?"

"It says here that he was careless and got hurt, and tried to blame my company." The eyes flashed a blue streak to Pam.

"Is that all the report says?" Pam knew that if she would ever lose control, now would be the time.

"Basically. It does mention he lost the case."

"If that's all the report says, then your staff didn't do a very good job at all! Does it mention that he climbed up on a ladder to try to fix a light fixture that was threatening to fall and hurt, or maybe kill, some of your employees? Does it mention that a work order had been turned in to your maintenance staff two weeks in a row, and nothing had been done about it? Does it mention that one of your maintenance staff bumped the ladder that Tom was standing on and knocked him off, causing major damage to his back? And Mrs. Bainbridge, does the report mention that Tom only sued for the exact amount that the doctors quoted him for the surgery?" Pam choked, tears threatening to spill from her eyes.

"Go on," the voice directed, a little softer now.

"Mrs. Bainbridge, I don't give a flying flip about your money for myself. I just want my brother's life back. I just want justice done. He's confined to a wheelchair, in so much pain he can't hold down a job. Your insurance company dropped him when your company fired him, and no other insurance company will touch him. We can't find a doctor that will do the surgery, because we don't have insurance. We can't get prescription drugs, because we don't have a doctor. And even if we could afford correct drugs for the pain, I don't know if he could hold down a job."

"It says here that you work two jobs. Tell me about them."

"I work from eight a.m. until five p.m. as office manager at a small law firm, Winger and Thomas. Then I work from six-thirty p.m. until nine p.m. cleaning offices in the building where my office is."

"That's some pretty long hours. Would you quit those jobs if you were awarded my money?"

"No. I enjoy my work—although," Pam added, as an after-thought, with a small smile playing with the corners of her mouth, "I might quit the cleaning job. That kind of hurts my own back."

Again, the cackling laugh ripped through the room.

"Do you have documentation of Tom's lawsuit and records of all the transactions?"

"I have records of everything that was ever said or done," Pam answered, almost daring to hope. "I can get them to you today by courier, if you'd like to see them."

"You really aren't easily daunted, are you?"

"Not when I believe I'm right about something." Pam stared directly into the blue fire across the desk from her.

Fiona Bainbridge held Pam's direct gaze for what seemed an eternity, but Pam was determined not to let her eyes waver.

Finally the older woman smiled and broke the stare. "I'll be in touch with you in a few days. I'll let you know one way or the other what I decide in your case."

Wanting to say more, but not wanting to push her luck, Pam reluctantly got up from her chair, wondering how to go about ending the interview. But the question was answered for her as Fiona Bainbridge suddenly swiveled her chair around to face the window. Once again, Pam was staring at the high back of the oversized leather chair.

Rude old bitch, Pam thought, as she turned and left the room.

It took Pam a while to fight the Dallas traffic, but finally back at the office of Winger & Thomas, she found a note on her desk that Tom had called. In fact, he had called twice. Drat! She hadn't wanted him to know she wasn't at work, and she definitely didn't want him to know *where* she was.

"Jan," she called to the receptionist who sat just outside her door, "did Tom sound okay when he called?"

Immediately, Jan appeared at Pam's door. "Yes, just a little irritated."

"So what's new?" Pam regretted the words as soon as they were out, but Jan knew her situation, and sympathized with her.

"I know. I remember when Tom used to call here and joke around with me, but now he acts like a different person. Even when I try to joke with him, he doesn't respond."

"Oh well, I guess I'd better call and see what he wants." Resignation sounded in Pam's voice. The morning had been draining, and she wasn't looking forward to having to explain anything to Tom.

"Tom, it's me, are you okay?" she asked when he picked up the phone.

"Pam, you need to come home right now!"

Panic clutched Pam. "Tom, are you okay?" she demanded into the phone.

"Just get home!" The receiver went dead.

Pam had never heard that tone in Tom's voice. And he definitely never *demanded* anything of her. He didn't sound sick. He sounded furious. Great! He must have found out where she'd been this morning.

Slowly opening the door to the apartment, Pam reluctantly went inside. What she saw made her mouth drop open. Tom sat at the small dinette table, which was covered in bottles of medicine. He was holding a piece of paper in his hand.

"What have you done, Pam?" His question shot across the room at her. The look on his face told her it was going to be a long afternoon.

Reluctantly, she went to the table and sat down. Little bottles, which appeared to be samples of pain medicine, covered the table.

She took the piece of paper from Tom and glanced over it. There were clear directions on when and how to take each medicine, and a chart to keep up with how each one affected Tom's pain, and if there were any adverse reactions to any of them, he was to call the doctor immediately.

The receipt on the sack that the medicine was delivered in was from the Bainbridge Medical Center, the in-house medical clinic that cared for Bainbridge Corporation employees. A note was attached that instructed Tom to try the samples and see which one helped his pain the most, and to let the doctor know, and that particular prescription would be supplied at no cost.

A slow smile spread across Pam's face. She couldn't believe this. Even if they didn't get the Bainbridge inheritance, at least Tom would get some pain relief.

"You know we have to send this back." Tom's bitter voice broke her reverie.

She simply could not believe her ears. And she'd had enough. No more would she put up with this martyr act Tom had fallen into. She took his hand in hers and gently looked into his eyes, but her voice wasn't gentle.

"Tom Spencer, you *will* try these pills. You *will* see which one helps your pain. And if you refuse, I'll shove them one by one down your throat, or up your butt! Whichever you prefer, but you *will take them*. At least you're kind of under a doctor's care now, and I won't let you blow this. If this is all we can get from Bainbridge Corporation, by damn, we'll take it!

The shrill ringing interrupted Pam's tirade. "Hello," she almost shouted into the phone.

"My, my, Miss Spencer, you do have a nice phone presence." Fiona Bainbridge's slightly amused voice came through the phone line.

"Oh, I'm so sorry," Pam quickly apologized. "Tom and I were just having a small discussion."

"I suppose he received the medicine?"

"Yes, and thank you so much."

"I suppose he wanted to send it back and tell me where to shove it?"

"I do think that crossed his mind," Pam answered honestly.

The cackle on the other end of the line was becoming familiar to Pam.

"Put him on the phone, please."

Pam handed the phone to Tom, who took it, not knowing who was on the other end.

"Tom Spencer," he stated, then sat and listened as the color slowly drained from his face.

Pam was going crazy wondering what Fiona Bainbridge could possibly be saying to Tom that could cause that look on his face and not have him hang up the phone on her.

Finally he placed the receiver back on the phone base, but continued to stare at it for the longest time.

"What?" Pam couldn't stand the tension any longer.

When Tom looked up at her, she saw a look in his eyes that she hadn't seen since before he'd had his accident. There was actually hope in his eyes, and a tear slid out the corner of one of them.

"Tom! What did she say to you? Please! I'm going crazy here!"

"I'm to experiment with the pain medicine the rest of the week and through the weekend, and Monday, I'm to report back to my old job. She says she sees no reason why I can't perform my duties as the supervisor of the department in a wheelchair, but she does expect me to stay off of ladders." Sudden laughter exploded from Tom for the first time in many, many months.

Pam dropped her head onto her folded arms and wept with happiness.

Chapter 2

"**Fifi, what the hell have you done this time?**" Everyone seated at the huge, formal dining table turned their heads in unison to stare at the formidable voice.

"Ah, Reese! I wondered how long it would take Sharon to alert you to my business." Fiona's flashing blue eyes held challenge as she greeted the man who leaned casually against the doorframe, his crossed arms emphasizing his wide chest.

Captivating. That was the only word Pam could think of to describe him. At least six feet tall, with coal black, slightly wavy hair with just a touch of gray beginning in the temples. Not handsome in the classic sense, but there was a presence, an aura, surrounding him, demanding that you pay attention.

The same blue eyes flashing from a tanned face held and met Fiona's challenge. "Well, someone at Bainbridge Corporation needs to keep me informed of your daft actions."

"Daft! How dare you walk in here and start insulting your grandmother, when I haven't seen you in over a year?"

"Fifi, you know my job takes me away for long periods at a time," he said, and seated himself at the large table. "Hello, Suzy," he warmly greeted the middle-aged housekeeper as she hurried out with a place setting for him. He took her hand in his and kissed it as she finished laying his silverware.

"It's good to have you home," she whispered with a smile. Obviously the two cared deeply for each other.

"Ahem!" Fiona's irritated sound broke up the short reunion, and Suzy hurried back to the kitchen.

Pam glanced over at Tom, who winked at her. He was apparently enjoying the commotion. He had become more and more like he used to be since returning to his job at Bainbridge Corporation. His insurance had been reinstated, and the company doctor had him on a pain medicine that seemed to relieve most of the discomfort in his back. Pending surgery was not far in the future, and each time she saw him beam his beautiful smile at her, Pam was reassured that she had done the correct thing when she answered Fiona Bainbridge's ad.

"So these are the freeloaders?" The new arrival penned Pam with his intense blue glare. His eyes were the exact same blue as his grandmother's, but seemed even more fierce radiating from his tanned face. Pam had a hard time holding his gaze, but was determined not to back down.

"Now, Reese, these are my house guests, and you *will* treat them with respect," Fiona directed.

"But this is *my* house, and I don't recall inviting these people to stay in *my* house." The tanned face seemed to darken just the slightest.

"Reese Bainbridge! How dare you talk to me like that in front of guests! You know very well this is my house for as long as I live! It only becomes your property on the day I die, and if I can help it that will be a long time from now."

"I'm sorry, Fifi. I may have crossed the line with that statement, but dammit, surely you can see how frustrating it was for me to get a copy of that stupid Public Notice you ran, advertising for a *worthy* heir. Don't you know how dangerous that could be? You've left yourself open to all kinds of shysters." His eyes stopped on Tom, as if seeing him for the first time. "Oh, this is perfect! A wheelchair always gets sympathy!" The laugh that exploded from his throat held no humor.

"Reese! That's quite enough. You and I can discuss this later, but right now we're going to try to have a civil dinner."

Pamela and Tom had been at Bainbridge Hall for a week. Fiona Bainbridge had approached them with an arrangement to which they had reluctantly agreed. They were to live in her home for one year, and if they met her qualifications, at the end of the year she would make them heirs to her estate.

Now, watching the exchange between Reese Bainbridge and his grandmother, Pam had the uneasy feeling that she and Tom were just being used to manipulate the wayward grandson to come home and fight for what was rightfully his. All of a sudden she felt like the bait for a trap, and a cold apprehension of problems ahead settled over her.

But she could face whatever lay ahead if it meant Tom would have his back surgery and be able to have a normal life. That's all she had ever wanted from Fiona Bainbridge, anyway.

After dinner, Reese and Fiona headed for the huge library to "discuss" the situation. Tom was in the room he had been assigned to, on the ground floor, so Pamela decided to take a stroll around the grounds.

Bainbridge Hall was a huge antebellum home built by Fiona's great-grandfather in the 1800s. But, as Fiona had pointed out as she gave Pam and Tom their tour, the house would not be part of the estate in question, as it was to go to her grandson at the time of her death.

As Pam rounded the west corner of the house, she stopped abruptly, captivated by the sunset. It was one of those rare East Texas sunsets that illuminated the entire sky with dazzling colors of all tints. As she stood and gazed at the changing hues, she became aware of voices, and realized she was hearing Fiona and Reese.

She had inadvertently stopped under a library window, which, apparently, someone had opened to take advantage of the unusually cool spring day. The terrain was lower at this point, so she couldn't be seen by the two people inside.

"So what stump did you find those two under?" She could detect the contempt in Reese Bainbridge's voice even from her distance.

"Here's their file. I've had detailed research done on them. They aren't scum, as you want to believe. Tom Spencer was employed by Bainbridge Corporation for ten years, and had an immaculate work record. As you can see, he was hurt on the job, and as far as I'm concerned, our little company screwed him. He was trying to fix a faulty light fixture that could have fallen and actually killed someone.

He did us a great favor, and we rewarded him by firing him for being careless, when in actuality it was one of our maintenance men who knocked him off the ladder. He's been in that chair for over a year now, and according to Dr. Ross, he's been in severe pain."

"Okay. But why do they have to live here? You could have done all that needs to be done for this Tom person without moving the two of them in here. Is the woman his wife?" Some of the sarcasm had left his voice, but Pam still detected a slight loathing.

"No. Pamela is Tom's sister. She's the one who answered my ad in the paper. She just wants to help her brother."

"Of course. I'm sure she's such a goody-two-shoes that she has no interest in the Bainbridge fortune. All she wants is to help her lil' ol' brother get out of that nasty ol' wheelchair." Pam shuddered at the raw contempt in his voice as he mimicked her.

"Actually, Reese, I do believe that's all she's interested in. And that's the only reason I'm considering them. She seems totally unimpressed with my money." Pam could have hugged Fiona for taking up for her.

"Fifi, I've never met a woman who was unimpressed with money. This one has the wool pulled so far over your eyes that you can't see the light. But you will. She'll show her true colors if given enough time and temptation."

"She's different from the women you associate with, Reese. That's the other reason I chose her. She's real and warm and loves her brother. Also, she looks different than the women you usually carouse with, so I knew you wouldn't be trying to get her into the sack as soon as you saw her." Fiona's familiar cackle wafted through the window, and Pam's face turned a slow red.

So that's what Fiona had meant in that first interview when she'd said Pam looked perfect. Fiona believed that because Pam wasn't a size six, Reese wouldn't find her attractive, and wouldn't pursue her.

Pam moved quietly from her vantage point and made her way to the edge of the large swimming pool. Slipping her shoes off and sitting on the edge of the pool, she dangled her feet in the cool water and contemplated the conversation she had just overheard. She should never have stood there and eavesdropped on their conversation, but she'd been so caught up in what they were saying she hadn't realized what she was doing until Fiona dropped the bombshell about her size.

It was true. Pam wasn't the typical size six—or smaller—that so many women tried to be, but that had never been a problem for her. She'd been told on many occasions that she had a voluptuous body, and her hourglass-type figure had always attracted more than her fair share of men. She was active, exercised regularly, was in perfect health, and enjoyed her body just the way it was.

So why would Fiona Bainbridge assume Reese wouldn't find her attractive? Did he have a problem with full-figured women? Well, Pam might have to change both their minds about that subject. A mischievous smile toyed with the corners of her full lips as a plan started to take root in her mind.

She wasn't blind. She knew her peridot green eyes, golden blonde hair, and Marilyn Monroe body type were a striking combination. Okay, so her body was somewhat larger than Marilyn's had been, but she'd been told she could pass as a double for the late actress. And although she wasn't vain, she knew what kind of reaction she got from the male population. She knew heads turned when she entered a room, and whispers passed appreciating lips. She also knew part of that reaction was due to her self-confident attitude and the fact that she liked who she was. That kind of attitude always set a person apart as appearing special.

She also knew that if Reese Bainbridge was a heterosexual male, he'd find her attractive to some extent, even if he never admitted it.

"Making yourself at home?" Pam was startled from her reverie by the question shot at her from the approaching figure of Reese Bainbridge.

Watching him casually move towards her like a big cat on the prowl, Pam prepared herself for his onslaught, determined not to let him intimidate her.

"Any reason I shouldn't?" she asked. His approach brought him so close he almost stepped on her hand, which was braced on the side of the pool beside her. She refused to look up at him because she knew that's what he wanted, from his towering vantage point above her.

"Rest assured, there are several reasons you and your brother shouldn't make yourselves at home here. But the main one is that this is not now, nor will ever be your home." Did the man ever speak without some form of sarcasm in his voice?

"Oh, Reese, I wouldn't be so sure of that if I were you." Pam couldn't resist the sudden urge to taunt this arrogant man.

Suddenly Reese wasn't towering above her any longer. Instead he had squatted, placing her almost between his legs, and when she swiveled her head around to look at him, their faces were less than six inches apart. "Now you listen to me, and you listen good." His breath, carrying a faint touch of mint, fanned the hair around her face as he spoke. "This is my home, and I'll have you and your freeloading brother out of here as soon as I can. You'll be back in that two-bedroom apartment where the two of you belong."

Whatever response his actions were intended to have on Pam was not, she was sure, what she actually felt. For the first time in her life, she felt engulfed by masculinity. Sensual, arousing, stimulating masculinity. Instead of feeling intimidated she felt breathtakingly alive, but she didn't dare let him sense her response to him. She was sure that was the way most women responded. And she most definitely didn't want him to know she fell into the same category.

"Are you sure, Reese?" she asked sweetly. "You might be begging me to stay in this house with you, before it's over."

"That'll be a cold day in hell," he hissed, his cold blue eyes trying to bore a hole into her calm green ones.

"Stranger things have happened," she warned, never wavering from his look.

He raked his eyes down her body, from the top of her short blonde hair to where her feet disappeared into the water, letting his eyes rest momentarily on her full breasts, before looking again into her eyes. "No, nothing that strange has ever happened," he assured her, before rising and walking away.

Pamela sat still, too drained to move. Her rapid heartbeat vibrated her entire body. This wasn't going to be easy. The man affected every part of her emotional being. But most of all, he had thrown down a challenge. Pam loved challenges. And she loved bringing arrogant men to their knees.

Because most arrogant men were actually just bullies, and when they were challenged, they usually wound up being cowards in disguise, just like the typical schoolyard bully. But Reese Bainbridge was a different breed. He wasn't going to be as easy to bring down as most. But she *would* bring him down. She'd have him eating from her hands before it was over. But she had to be careful. Those feelings she'd just experienced had never been present with anyone else, and she couldn't afford to get caught in her own trap.

Yes, this one was dangerous, but that just made the game more exciting. Adrenaline charged through her. She was ready for the battle.

Back in the room that had been his since childhood, Reese collapsed into a huge recliner by the window. What had just happened? He had used some of his most intimidating work on that woman out by the pool, and she hadn't wavered. Hadn't seemed to have gotten his point at all.

But, he, on the other hand, had almost been lost in those strange green eyes. Fifi was right. This woman was different from any he had ever met. He could tell that, and he'd only just met her. Fifi was also right about her not looking like the women he usually dated. But the women he usually dated were politically correct. They were the type to be seen with in this society. What Fifi didn't know was that those women didn't do a thing for his libido. Oh, sure, he found one occasionally who turned him on enough to have a fling with, but the excitement soon turned to boredom. Fifi didn't know about his secret fascination for the Marilyn Monroe, Jane Mansfield body types, and that at the back of his closet was a stash of magazine articles and posters he'd collected as a teenage boy and young man.

Fifi also didn't know that this Pam Spencer was the most sensual, sexy woman he had ever met in person. And that if it meant moving heaven and earth, he had to have her out of this house. He didn't think he could stand that kind of temptation every day. And he sure as hell wasn't going to get involved with some scheming user who thought she could just waltz into his life and take what was rightfully his.

Or *did* Fifi know all of this?

The thought struck him like a lightning bolt. Had she somehow discovered his fascination for a woman with lush curves, and was playing him for a fool? Was this her way to lure him home, and possibly back into the family business?

He leaped from the chair and headed to the back of his walk-in closet, to his secret hiding place. It had been a long time since he'd looked through his collection, but he remembered exactly where he kept it hidden. Pulling a panel from the back of the wall, he used a flashlight to peer into the secret nook he'd created when he was thirteen, just for his collection of magazines, pictures and posters.

It was empty! Anger shot through him like a dagger. How dare his grandmother plunder his property! These articles and pictures were becoming more and more valuable! Not that he needed the money, but the Marilyn Monroe memorabilia was a growing multimillion-dollar business, and he was sure some of the articles he had would bring quite a large sum at an auction.

But he couldn't let Fifi know right now that he was on to her. That would just play right into her hands. No, but the valuable knowledge he'd just gained would give him an upper hand in the battle in which he seemed to have found himself engaged.

With added determination to have Tom and Pam Spencer out of his house, Reese went to bed to spend a restless night.

Pam had kept both jobs after moving into Bainbridge Hall. Fiona had tried to encourage her to at least give up the cleaning job, but Pam refused.

She saw an opportunity to save all her money while they were at Bainbridge Hall with no bills to pay. When it was time to leave, she'd have a little nest egg to start over on.

Because in Pam's wildest dreams she never believed Fiona Bainbridge would leave her money and holdings to Tom and her. Especially after meeting the powerful Reese Bainbridge. She was sure Reese had ways of getting what he wanted. But she honestly didn't care as long as Tom's health was back to normal.

It was usually ten o'clock when she got home at the end of her day. Some days she was so tired she could barely drag herself to her room before collapsing into bed. This was one of those nights, and as she wearily closed the front door to Bainbridge Hall, she turned and almost ran squarely into Reese.

"You keep some late hours, don't you? What are you up to? Out seeing a boyfriend?"

It was the first time she'd seen him since their meeting beside the pool. Too tired to argue, Pam answered honestly, "No, I've been at work."

"In jeans and a T-shirt? I thought you worked in an office. Come on, Pamela, give me a little credit."

It was the first time he had called her by her name, and she liked the way it rolled off his tongue.

"I do work in an office during the day. Then at night I help clean the building the offices are in." Pam tried to step around him, but a strong hand shot out and caught her arm to stop her.

"I think you're lying through your teeth," he whispered, close to her face. Pam smelled liquor on his breath. So that was it. He'd been drinking and was ready for battle. Well, she was too tired tonight, so his little battle would have to wait.

"Let me go, Reese. If you think I'm lying, why don't you come to where I work, and find out," she said, and tried to pull away from him. But he tightened his grip and pulled her closer to him. Her breasts were brushing the front of his shirt.

"Stop it! You're hurting my arm," she demanded weakly, as she watched, mesmerized, his lips lowering toward hers.

Not able to move even if she'd wanted to, Pam felt Reese's hold on her arm become gentler as his lips covered hers. She would just let him kiss her, then maybe he'd let her go. But as soon as his lips touched hers a bolt of awareness shot through her like nothing she had ever experienced before, leaving her weak down to her very bones. Not wanting to, she felt herself sagging against his wide chest as his arms pulled her closer. One of his legs wedged between hers. Her lips parted slightly to allow his tongue to gently tug and trace the full curve of her bottom lip. Timidly she touched her tongue to his, which seemed to ignite him. She felt his hand slip under her shirt and up her ribcage to stop just beneath her breast, while his thumb gently moved back and forth on the tender skin.

But abruptly he ended the kiss and stepped back from her. She staggered from the unexpected release, and from the weakened state she was in.

"This is exactly what you want, isn't it? Trap me in your little scheme, just like you trapped Fifi. Well, you can forget that!" He turned and bounded up the stairs, leaving Pam shaken and confused.

How dare that jerk! Attack her as soon as she walked in the door, and then try to act as if it were her fault. She was coming to the conclusion that rich people were lacking in a few major brain functions.

After spending a restless, sleepless night, Pam dressed for work the next morning and headed to the kitchen to get a cup of strong coffee to take to work with her.

As soon as she entered the door to the kitchen she spotted Reese at the coffee pot, pouring himself a cup. She was about to turn and leave when he spotted her.

"Pam, can we talk for a moment?" A note of perplexity resounded in his voice. "Can I pour you a cup of coffee?"

Well, this was surely a change. Reese Bainbridge being civil to her.

"Sure," she agreed, laying her purse on the counter top, and taking the cup of coffee he handed her.

"Look." He almost seemed embarrassed. "About last night. I'm really sorry. I'd had too much to drink, and I got out of hand. I really do apologize. I'm not a real cad, I just act like it sometimes." His gaze held hers, and she caught a glimpse of another side of Reese Bainbridge.

"Apology accepted," Pam said. She turned with her coffee and picked up her purse.

"That's it? That's all you have to say?"

"I'm already late for work, Reese. I really do have to go. Don't worry about last night. It was nothing." *Big liar,* she accused herself, as she pulled the door closed behind her.

At six-thirty p.m. sharp, Pam, having changed from the dress and heels she'd worn to work into a pair of jeans and T-shirt, stepped out of the utility closet in the hallway, pulling her cleaning cart behind her. One of the dust cloths fell off and she stooped for it, just as it was swept up by a tanned hand with just a sprinkling of dark hair dusting the back and knuckles.

27

Startled, she quickly stood and found herself looking into the blazing blue eyes of Reese Bainbridge.

"So you weren't lying, after all." An amused smile lifted one corner of his mouth.

"What are you doing here?" she demanded.

"You told me to come check on you if I didn't believe you."

"So you thought I was lying?"

"Let's just say I couldn't believe any woman would keep holding down two jobs if she had hopes of getting her hands on the Bainbridge fortune."

"You really do have a low opinion of women, don't you?"

"Most of them."

"Well, I don't know who hurt you, but it wasn't me, so don't keep taking your nasty attitude out on me. If you don't mind, now, I have work to do." She made an attempt to push her cart up the hallway, but his large hand reached out and stopped it.

"Why are you doing this?" he asked. "Are you trying to impress on Fiona that you're really a hard working person and you sincerely don't care about her money?"

She was about to tell him that she never expected to see any of the Bainbridge money when she stopped herself. Why let him know she thought he'd win the battle in the long run?

"Actually, Reese, I'm not trying to impress anyone of anything. I just do this for the exercise. It doesn't cost as much as going to a gym."

A low chuckle rumbled from his wide chest.

"You know, you could still be scamming me. I want to watch you work to see if you really do clean these offices."

"Oh, I don't think so!" she exploded. "I'll call security and have you thrown out if you don't leave right now! You've got to be the most frustrating man I have ever known!"

"Have you known a lot of men, Pam?" Suddenly his voice was soft and insinuating.

"John!" she yelled toward the front of the building, where the security desk was. It didn't take long for an older man in a uniform to come around the corner.

"Are you okay, Miss Spencer? Oh, hello, Boss, I see everything's under control." And he turned and headed back to his desk.

"Boss?" she squeaked.

"Yes. Bainbridge Corporation owns the security company that handles this building."

"Well, of course. Why am I not surprised?" So he'd known all along she wasn't lying. All he had to do was ask the security guard. He just wanted to harass her. Pam had an urge to smack the superior smile off his mouth. Or maybe kiss it. *Where had that come from?*

Needing to break the spell that just looking at his mouth had cast upon her, Pam clutched the handle of the cart and forcefully pushed it down the hall. "I have work to do. Watch if it pleases you, I don't care." She hoped her challenge would discourage him, but to her dismay she realized he was following slightly behind her.

As they reached the elevators, Reese stopped her. "I'm leaving now. And incidentally, for your information, I've never been hurt by a woman, because I don't let them get close enough to hurt me."

"Until now, you mean?" Pam smiled sweetly. She shot the challenge at him as the elevator doors swooshed closed on the astonished look on his face.

Chapter 3

Come in!" Pam barely heard the command through the thick oak door. Expectantly, she pushed the door open to find Fiona Bainbridge sitting at a huge desk, just like at Bainbridge Corporation. But the setting was much more relaxed here in her home office.

Family pictures hung on the wall and were arranged on the bookshelves. Small *objets d'art*, obviously expensive, and other artsy–crafty items were also scattered around.

For some reason these surroundings made Fiona Bainbridge seem more like "real people" to Pam, and her eyes held a softness when they finally rested on the small woman who carried such a large impact.

"You like my office?" Fiona asked, unexpectedly.

"Yes!" Pam's voice held her obvious surprise. "It's a lot different than the one at Bainbridge Corporation. A lot less like an institution."

The cackling laugh always overwhelmed Pam a little. Fiona was usually so serious that when she did laugh it was astonishing how her face lit up, and the sound itself was a surprise, too.

"I've really got to spend more time with you, Pamela. I like your honesty. You're not intimidated by me and my millions. Are you intimidated by Reese?"

Pam's eyes sliced back to the small frame sitting across the desk from her. Why was Fiona asking her something like this? She was suddenly on guard.

"Come, sit and relax." Fiona directed Pam to a sitting area arranged in front of an extensive fireplace. The plush leather couch seemed to swallow Fiona's small frame as she settled into it and motioned for Pam to sit on the matching couch across from her. "I need to talk to you. To get to know you better."

Does this have to do with my worthiness to inherit your millions? Pam wanted to ask.

"I need to be around someone young and full of spunk, like you. Sometimes I think I'm shriveling up into an old prune. Look at us. You look like a fresh, plump grape, and I'm an old, dried out raisin." Totally out of character, Fiona ran her hand across her wrinkled arm, giving Pam a glance of the real woman sitting before her. A real person, concerned about real things like getting old and wrinkled.

"Ms. Bainbridge—"

"Oh, please, call me Fiona." She interrupted Pam with a wave of her hand. "Fiona." Pam felt strange addressing her in such a personal way, but Fiona seemed to want to get personal this morning. "Fiona, don't talk about yourself like that. You should never think or say negative things about yourself."

"This isn't negative, girl, it's the truth."

"But you compared yourself with me. You shouldn't do that." This was a soapbox Pam was always ready to climb up on.

"Life is so strange," Fiona continued. "When I was a teenager, back in the '30s, women your size were considered the beautiful ones. I hated my size. I wanted to be as large as I felt my brain was. I always felt like my full-size brain was stuck in this pint-size body, and that my body hindered my brain from doing the things it was capable of doing. So I guess I overcompensated and became a real bitch, just trying to cover the fact that I'm so small."

"You may not know it, but a lot of fat people feel the same way on a reversed basis," Pam said.

"You mean they feel like their body is hindering what their brain wants to do?"

"Exactly," Pam said. "But my contention is, the brain is who we really are. The body is just the vehicle, and each vehicle is different, and in being different, each vehicle is limited to some extent. For instance, a tall person can't do some of the things you can do, just like you can't do some of the things a tall person can do. The same goes for anyone, whether they're tall, short, skinny, fat, or whatever."

"Well, that does make sense," Fiona acknowledged. "I don't guess I ever thought it through like that."

"That's why," Pam continued, "we should never judge each other by the vehicle, or package if you will, because if all of our brains were taken out and placed on a shelf, there would be no short, tall, fat, or skinny brains. Or for that matter, no different-colored brains. They would all pretty much look the same."

"Or old ones," Fiona added.

"That's right," Pam agreed, laughing.

"Why didn't you come into my life before now?" Fiona asked, wistfully. "You could have really helped me see myself in a different light."

"It's not too late," Pam encouraged. "It's never too late to change the way you think about yourself. Just stop thinking the negative thoughts and replace them with positive ones. And besides that, look at you. You're a success in life. You own and run a large corporation, you're filthy rich, and live in a mansion. So many women would switch places with you!"

"But I'm not happy," Fiona admitted.

"Then get happy," Pam said.

"What? Just like that? You tell me to get happy?" Fiona looked at Pam as if she'd taken leave of her senses. "I've had too many years of unhappiness to just snap my fingers and make it all go away." A touch of bitterness crept into her voice.

"I know it won't happen overnight, but happiness is mostly just a state of mind," Pam insisted. "If the average person put the two of us together, with our life's situations, they'd think you'd be the happy one because you have everything. But I'm the happy one, even though in comparison to you, I have nothing."

"Why are you happy?"

"Because I've chosen to be. I don't dwell on the things that make me unhappy. And if something is making me unhappy, I try to change it."

"Like applying for an old woman's fortune to help your brother?"

The question took Pam off guard momentarily, but she quickly recovered. "Exactly," she said without apology.

"What about Reese?" Again, an unexpected question.

"What about him?"

"Does he make you unhappy?"

Pam had no idea where this line of talk would take them, but she'd been totally honest with Fiona up until this point, so why change now? "Your grandson is a jerk. He makes me very unhappy, so I stay as far away from him as I can."

Fiona laughed so hard she went into a coughing attack. When she recovered, she fastened her flashing blue eyes on Pam and said, "If I could have searched the world over, I could never have found a person as perfect for Reese as you are. Most women fall at his feet in adoration, but not you. Oh, yes, this is going to be *soooo* good."

"Fiona, what are you talking about?" Pam's voice was sharp with apprehension.

"Nothing. Look," she blatantly changed the subject, "I really need to get some work done, even though it's Saturday. But I've thoroughly enjoyed this visit we've had. I'm going to think about the things we've discussed and see if I can change my outlook on life."

"Fiona," Pam started.

"Go. Go find Reese and give him hell." Fiona dismissed Pam with a wave of her hand as she returned to her desk with an unusually big grin on her face.

Stunned. That's the only word that could describe Pam's feelings as she stood outside the closed door to the powerful Fiona Bainbridge's office. What had just happened in there? Had she really given Fiona advice on life?

"Been in there trying to make some Brownie points?" Reese's sarcastic question preceded him down the hallway as he made his way toward her.

Pam hadn't seen him since the night at the office when she'd let her tongue overlap her good judgment and thrown that stupid challenge at him about being attracted to her.

Suddenly she had the urge to run away and not face him this morning. As she was about to turn in the opposite direction, he caught her arm.

"Not so fast. You're not going anywhere until you hear me out on a few things."

Reese's masculine aftershave settled around Pam, enveloping her in an imaginary, sensuous film, making her feel as if she were becoming one with him. An unfamiliar weakness stole over her, taking away the strength she usually possessed.

"Like what?" she managed without stammering.

"Come into my office," he directed, still clutching her arm and leading her to a door across the hall from Fiona's office.

"Oh, two offices in one morning! Don't I feel special!" Pam tried to sound flippant as Reese led her into an office the same size as Fiona's. This one definitely lacked any feminine touches. Instead, one wall was lined with shelves full of books, while the rest of the walls were covered with photographs of a wide variety of wild animals, birds, and creatures that Pam couldn't name.

"You should feel damn special," Reese charged, as he closed the door behind them.

Feeling a real battle brewing, Pam turned her full attention to Reese. "Meaning?" she challenged.

"Meaning, I still can't believe you've schemed your way into this house, and apparently, you're actually getting to Fiona, which is hard to believe, since she's so cold-blooded."

Remembering Fiona's mandate to give Reese hell, Pam smiled sweetly at him. "And am I getting to you yet, Reese?" she asked, perching on the corner of his desk and looking coyly up at him.

Swiftly he was there, wedging one of his legs between hers and penning her to the desk. If she tried to get away from him, she'd be sitting astraddle his leg.

"Don't play with me, woman. You're just a little girl when it comes to men like me. And, besides that, I've already told you, you're not my type."

"Have you ever made love to a real woman?" Pam dared to whisper, mesmerized by the closeness of his lips. Lips that were slowly lowering to hers.

Pam melted against Reese's broad chest as he pulled her close and formed his firm lips over hers, which were soft and supple. She felt her skirt slipping up over her thighs as he slid her off the desk to straddle the leg that was still wedged firmly between hers. She'd never known anything so erotic! She felt her excitement rising as Reese continued gently exploring her mouth. Her breasts heaved against his chest with each panting breath she took.

"Oops!" The voice and the closing door brought the two people back to their senses. As they stared at the door, the cackling laugh drifting down the outside hallway told them who had caught them kissing.

"Damn her!" Reese swore, stepping quickly away from Pam. She would have staggered if the desk hadn't been there for support.

"Well, it's obvious by your reactions you've never made love to a real man," he threw at Pam as he went behind his desk and sat down.

Adjusting her clothes and her dignity, Pam turned to face him.

"Did you bring me in here to maul me, or did you want to talk about something in particular?" she asked, proud of the seemingly undisturbed sound of her voice.

With his eyes fixed on her, Reese leaned back in the huge brown leather chair and a crooked smile turned one corner of his mouth to an upward angle. In this light, his face looked like chiseled stone in which someone had stuck blue diamonds in the eye sockets. The brilliant blue eyes set in that tan, perfectly carved face gave him a surreal look. There was an untamed wildness about him that Pam had never noticed before.

"You know, when I think about it, you and Fiona do deserve each other. You're both bitches. I don't know why I don't just pack my bags and leave, and let you two have at it. But for some reason I can't bring myself to make it that easy on the two of you. No," he mused, steepling his fingers together in front of his mouth. "No, it will be a lot more fun to see this thing through. I can't wait to see both of you squirming in defeat."

"Why do you hate your grandmother?" Pam's question came unexpectedly to both of them. "I can understand why you'd resent me, but why your grandmother?"

"I don't hate Fifi. I really do love the old gal, but I have to stand up for what I believe, or I'll wind up dead at an early age, just like my father."

"I don't understand."

"My grandfather, Earl Bainbridge, started Bainbridge Corporation when my dad was a baby. Granddad was a success in any business venture he tried, but Bainbridge Corporation was the success of a lifetime. As it grew, it added wealth to the wealth he had inherited from his father. But the long hours and stress put a strain on Granddad's heart, and he died when my dad was in his late teens." Reese paused, as if finished, but Pam sat expectantly waiting, and he continued.

"As soon as my dad was out of college, Fifi bullied him into taking over the running of Bainbridge Corporation, even though he desperately wanted to pursue another course in life. His dream was to be an airplane pilot. He was fascinated with flying, but to my knowledge, he never got to take a single lesson." Bitterness edged Reese's voice as he warmed up to unpleasant memories.

"So what happened?" Pam prompted.

"Every night, he came home unhappy and miserable. So many nights I would lie in my bed and listen to my mother cry and beg him to leave this town and pursue the dream that would make him happy. But he just couldn't stand up to Fiona. So my mom left instead. She said she couldn't stand to stay and watch him die a slow death."

"She just left? She left you, too?" Suddenly, Pam had a small insight into part of the reason Reese seemed so bitter.

"She promised she'd come back and get me after she got settled down, but fate had a different plan." Now, sadness replaced the bitter note in his voice.

"What happened?"

"Two months after she left, she was killed in a car accident."

Pam wondered why Reese Bainbridge was sharing his life's story with her, but she didn't have to wait long for the answer.

"My dad really threw himself into his work, then two years later he had a heart attack, just like Granddad, and died."

"Oh, Reese—"

"No! I'm not looking for your sympathy. I'm simply explaining to you why Fiona's and my relationship is as it is. Why she has supposedly disowned me. You see, after my father died, I made a promise to myself. I vowed that I would never, and I mean *never* work at Bainbridge Corporation. And as you might guess, that didn't set too well with Fiona. She was determined that this was a family-owned and family-run business. She said that if I didn't promise to work for the business, she wouldn't put me through college to get a degree in something that I wasn't meant to do. So I told her, in no uncertain terms, to run the business herself, and I proceeded to work my way through college and get my degree in journalism and photography."

So that's what all the photos are, Pam acknowledged to herself.

"Every time I come home for a visit," Reese continued, "we have this knock-down and drag-out fight about me 'quitting my roaming all over the world and coming home and doing what I was born to do.' So the last time, I told her I didn't know if I would ever come back again until she was dead."

At Pam's gasp, Reese fastened his eyes on her. "Does that sound harsh to you? Well, I'm sorry, but until you've had Fiona constantly nag at and harangue you for years, you really can't judge me, can you?"

Not knowing what to say, Pam sat just sat and looked at him.

"So, Pam, what I brought you in here to say this morning, is that you were right."

"About what?"

"I have been hurt by the only two women that were ever important in my life. One left me and the other one has turned me against her. I'd never really thought about it until you mentioned it the other night."

"So that's why you don't like women?"

"I never said I didn't like women. Women have their uses. But I don't think I'll ever give my heart to one. I plan to take real good care of my heart and live a lot longer than my father and grandfather did. So you're wasting your time if you think I'm going to fall for your little flirtatious acts."

Pam was taken off guard by Reese's swiftly turning the attention back to her. Before she could think of an answer, he stood and motioned for her to do the same. As she rose from the chair, Pam looked up to catch Reese's eyes glued to her breasts.

Realizing he'd been caught, the lopsided grin came back on his face. "You do have some interesting assets, I'll have to admit."

Pam brushed quickly past him and left the room, slamming the door closed behind her. She had to get away from this place for a while. This morning had been an emotional roller coaster and she needed to go somewhere and try to sort her thoughts out. She'd find Tom and see if he wanted to go to the park with her.

Back in his office, Reese tilted back in his chair.

Damn! Damn Fiona for discovering his number one and maybe only weakness and bringing her to live right here under his nose. Damn Pam for being so soft and sexy. And damn his mind and body for craving her on his every waking moment since he'd met her. This was going to be the hardest battle he'd ever fought, and he'd fought some tough ones.

But he would win. Reese Bainbridge took after his grandmother in his stubbornness. He always won his battles. Fifi should know that by now, so why was she still pushing so hard? What motive did she have? Did she think he'd give in and go to work at Bainbridge Corporation just so she'd change her mind about disowning him? Surely she knew him better than that after all these years.

Pam found Tom sitting in front of the laptop computer Fiona had furnished him to help him keep records for his work.

"What're you doing?" she asked, after coming through the open door.

"Oh, just going over some figures from the company."

"Working on Saturday? You know all work and no play makes Tom a dull boy."

"So what am I supposed to play, Pam? Wanna take me golfing?" The words were the same Tom would have used a few weeks ago, but almost all the bitterness was gone.

"I thought we might go to the park," Pam answered, not wanting to get into another confrontation. Two in one morning were quite enough.

"Thanks," he said, smiling at her. "But Fiona gave me this graph to go over and asked if I could project the earnings for next year. I know you don't want to hear this, but I really am grateful to her for giving me my job and, basically, my life back."

"I know, and although I feel she owes it to you, I'm grateful, too. But don't let her take advantage of you," she admonished, her mind still boggled from Reese's earlier revelations.

"I'm not. You want to know something?"

"What?"

"I always loved working at Bainbridge Corporation. It's one of the largest tool manufacturers in the nation, and I believe we put out a quality product."

Pam watched Tom's eyes light up just talking about his job, and realized for the first time that one of Tom's problems with being in his situation was that he had missed his work. She watched an amused smile playing on his lips and asked, "What's causing that 'cat that caught the mouse' look on your face?"

"Fiona said the strangest thing when she gave me these figures to go over. She told me to familiarize myself with as much as I could, because someday I might be running the place!"

"What did she mean?" Pam's interest level had shot up two-hundred-fold.

"I have no idea. When she said it, she was in the process of walking out the door, so I couldn't question her."

"Hmmm, that's really strange," Pam agreed.

"Anyway, thanks for the invite, but I'm in the middle of this and don't want to quit."

"Okay. I know a brush off when I hear it. I'm out of here."

"Love you," Tom called as she left the room.

A warm smile glowed on Pam's face as she walked outside onto the patio. It had been a long time since Tom had yelled "love you" to her when she was huffing out of a room. He used to always do that when he thought he'd upset her about something. Dear, wonderful Tom.

"You're looking real pleased with yourself." Reese's voice startled her out of her pleasant memories.

He sat in a corner chair. Pam hadn't seen him when she came outside.

"Just going over ways to get under your skin," she taunted him.

"Don't give yourself too much credit. As I said earlier, you don't have a chance."

"Trying to convince me or you?" she slung over her shoulder as she went down the steps and headed for the pool.

43

Since Tom wouldn't go to the park with her, she'd just go for a swim instead. Swimming always helped clear her mind. In the pool house she searched through the courtesy bathing suits that were kept for guests who might need one. She found a two-piece that she thought would fit and put it on. The bottom was fine, but the top, as usual, exposed a large expanse of bare breast. Oh well, she thought, no one would see her anyway.

She slid into the cool water and made several laps before stopping to take a rest. She was halfway up the steps that led out of the pool when she looked up and realized her nose was inches away from a pair of legs covered in a rug of curly dark hair. Sensing that she was staring at mid-thigh, she didn't dare raise her eyes any further, but slowly backed into the pool before lifting her eyes to Reese's blue challenge.

"I'm sure you didn't know that this is the time I swim every day, did you?" Amused sarcasm edged his voice.

"Actually, I didn't know you ever crawled out from under your rock long enough to get in the water." Pam's sugar-sweet voice belied the sting of her words.

Before she could guess his intentions, Reese jumped into the pool quite close to her, splashing water into her face. She was busily wiping water from her eyes when she felt two strong arms circling her waist from behind, and Reese's body being pressed close to her.

"So you think you can taunt a real man," his low voice vibrated close to her ear. "If you keep flaunting yourself in front of me, I might just show you how much trouble that could get you in."

"Flaunting?" Pam's voice trembled, partly from anger, and partly from the reaction of feeling his arms on her naked midriff.

"Yes, flaunting," Reese said, turning her to face him.

If having him this close from behind was disturbing, Pam realized, facing him at this close proximity was much worse. She watched his eyes settle on her exposed cleavage, which was even more exaggerated by the buoyancy of the water.

"What do you mean 'flaunt'? I was here first," she shot at him, trying to push away and get some distance between them. But he held her close with his fingers laced together at the back of her waist.

"Yes, but you knew I was coming," he insisted.

"You are the most arrogant, self-centered man I have ever met," she almost shouted. Now she had her hands on his shoulders, pushing at him with all her might. As she watched the amused grin grow larger, spreading across his face, she realized that her pushing motions were just emphasizing her breasts.

"Let me go!" she demanded between clenched teeth.

"Why? I'm rather enjoying myself. That's what you had in mind, wasn't it? Showing me all you have to offer?"

"Damn you!" she lashed out, not pushing anymore, but still having to rest her hands on his shoulders for lack of anywhere else to put them. "Why would I be trying to show you anything when you assured me I wasn't your type? I'm not that stupid."

He could deny being attracted to her all he wanted to, but Pam was sure he was captivated by his view, and she was sure she was feeling him respond to her as their bodies pressed together under the water. Suddenly she was filled with a sense of power.

"Or maybe," she smiled sweetly, "you just don't know what you really want."

"And maybe," he answered, just as sweetly, "you've never been burned from playing with fire."

But Pam was already burning as he lowered his lips and claimed hers. Her hands naturally slid up his shoulders and buried in his dark hair as he pulled her close and molded their bodies together.

Neither of them heard the cackling laugh nor saw the small figure watching from an upstairs window.

Chapter 4

Fiona Bainbridge turned from the window and clasped her hands together in delight. This plan was coming together almost faster than she could keep up! Just possibly, the best thing she had ever done for Bainbridge Corporation and for Reese was to place that ad in the paper.

Sometimes that boy just didn't know what was best for him. Okay, so he wasn't exactly a boy. But he'd always be that darling grandbaby who came into her life thirty-three years ago, and she wanted, whether he believed it or not, to see him happy before she checked out of this life. And she would even enjoy seeing a great-grandbaby or two.

And she was determined to make sure that Bainbridge Corporation was left in good hands.

This plan—this plan might just possibly make all of it happen.

The blazing blue eyes illuminated her small face, making her look ten years younger than her seventy-three years.

Pam quickly dried her hair, applied makeup, and dressed in a slinky purple pantsuit. Not bad, she thought, as she did a last minute check of herself in the full-length mirror that stood in her bedroom before she headed downstairs.

Fiona had called for a "family meeting" to take place at dinner tonight. That probably made Reese do a slow burn, Pam mused as she entered the library, where they were told to meet before dinner.

There were no lights on, and at first glance, the room looked empty. She must be the first one here.

"That sure is a self-satisfied smile, Miss Spencer. You really think you've got it made, don't you?"

It took Pam a few moments to spot the location of the low, caustic voice, but soon her eyes stopped on Reese, kicked back in a recliner with a drink in his hand.

"Meaning?" She wasn't about to give him the satisfaction of thinking she knew what he was referring to.

"You know very well what I mean. You walk through this house just thinking about all you have to gain by being here."

"I thought the house was yours. Why would I think I could lay claim on anything in it? Won't the contents go to you, too?"

"Of course." He hadn't moved, but Pam had the disturbing feeling that she could be pounced on at any moment. Tonight he seemed almost like one of those Bengal tigers she'd seen in the photos hanging in his office.

But at twenty-seven Pam had learned to never run from trouble. Even when she knew she should. Tonight was no different. She smelled trouble with a capital T, but that only caused her adrenalin to flow faster.

"Then if I want the house and contents, I guess I'll just have to seduce you, won't I, Reese?"

She never knew anyone could move so fast. He must have had a lot of practice running from the wild animals he photographed, because suddenly he was there, towering over her.

"Now you listen to me, and you listen good." He wasn't touching her, but she felt penned. Trapped by his blue glare. She couldn't have moved if she'd tried.

"I don't get *seduced* by women. Is that clear? *I* do the seducing, and that is only for the women *I* want. And *I* don't want you, Pamela Spencer. The sooner you get that through your head, the better off we'll all be."

"Dinner is ready," Suzy's hesitant voice called from the doorway. There was no doubt she'd heard his tirade.

"Where is everyone else, Suzy?" Reese asked, not moving an inch from Pam.

"What do you mean?" Suzy asked.

"This is supposed to be a *family* dinner," Reese answered, with heavy disdain on the "family" part.

"Miss Fiona said that she and Mr. Spencer were going out to dinner, and that I was supposed to prepare a cozy dinner for you and Miss Pam." Confusion sounded in Suzy's voice.

The distraction had given Pam the strength to move away from Reese. But suddenly he turned his blue glare to her.

"You knew about this, didn't you?"

What on earth had Fiona been thinking? Surely she knew this would backfire on her, but should Pam admit she was as surprised as

Reese, or should she play along with whatever Fiona had in mind? Her hesitation was all Reese needed.

"You did know! You were in on this with that scheming old bitch! That's why you wore that sexy outfit. You actually were going to try and seduce me, weren't you? You naïve little fool. You really have no idea who you're playing with, do you?"

And with that, he turned and stormed from the room. In a moment, the two women heard the front door slamming.

"Wh—what should I do about dinner?" Suzy seemed almost in tears.

"Have you eaten?" Pam asked.

"Why, no. I don't eat until everyone else has been served."

"Well, Suzy, it looks like it's just you and me, so why don't we go and enjoy that fine meal you've prepared."

"But, Miss Spencer—"

"Oh, please, just call me Pam, and come on, sit with me and tell me all about the crazy family that lives in this house."

Once Suzy relaxed, the two women had a long, leisurely dinner, with Suzy talking lovingly about a young Reese Bainbridge who had grown up under the stern, watchful eyes of Fiona Bainbridge. Of a young Reese Bainbridge who had talked to her, Suzy, when he needed the love and warmth of a real mother figure, and who had cried in her arms on many occasions because he missed his parents.

Pam went to sleep that night feeling compassion for Reese Bainbridge, instead of the hurt she should have felt because of all the harsh things he'd said to her earlier in the evening. But the last thing that her mind registered before sleep claimed her was Reese's voice accusing her of wearing a sexy outfit to seduce him. *Hmmm, so he thought it was sexy, huh?* She wore a small smile as sleep enveloped her.

The next morning Pam dressed for work and slipped quietly out the front door, skipping her usual morning cup of coffee. She didn't want to face anyone after last night's fiasco.

Her morning was progressing without any mishaps until she looked up and saw Sam Winger, the senior partner of Winger & Thomas, approaching her desk.

"Good morning, Pam, how are you?" His voice was too cheerful, and suddenly Pam was on guard.

"Just fine, Sam, and you?"

"Oh, better than I deserve," came his usual response. "Pam, you and Tom are living at the Bainbridge estate, aren't you?"

"Temporarily."

"Oh? I thought it was a permanent arrangement."

"I'm sure it's not, Sam, but why are you asking?"

"Well, um, well, the security service that we employ for this building has offered to clean our offices for free. They said we're one of their preferred customers and they want to do this for us. And I thought that since you don't have to pay rent and bills now, you don't really need the extra job. Hell, I'm surprised you've stayed on with us, at all. But, don't get me wrong, I don't know what we'd do if you left."

A deadly, numbing rage slowly crept over Pam. How could Reese Bainbridge stoop so low? This was revenge, pure and simple. Damn him! Okay, so she really would like to have quit the cleaning job, but she'd kept it because it was wonderful to see her bank account growing. Plus, she'd kept it partly to spite Reese. And now he'd made her lose it.

"Pam? Are you okay? You can keep the job if it's going to be a problem." Concern edged the older man's voice, and Pam realized her emotions must be apparent on her face.

"Oh, no, Sam, it's not a problem. I'll actually be glad to have a little extra time on my hands at night," she lied. To do what? Sit in her room and try to avoid that asshole Reese Bainbridge? Or to spend it trying to seduce him? A slow smile spread across her face. Yes! She'd bring him *down*! He'd told her she didn't know who she was messing with. Well, apparently, he didn't know who *he* was messing with. He had no idea how far Pam would go to win a battle. And this was most definitely a battle now. He had brought it on!

"Yes, I can see you're feeling pretty good about the situation, so I'll let you get back to work. And I'm serious, Pam, don't even think about leaving Winger & Thomas. You're very valuable to us."

Still smiling, Pam said, "Don't worry, Sam, I'm not going anywhere."

Pam's anger spurred her though the day, giving her extra energy to get more done than she'd expected to. But at times she'd find herself just staring into space, planning her revenge.

She left work early, and as much as she hated to, headed into the Dallas traffic. Even though it was only June, the East Texas heat was already making itself known. But it didn't take long to get to the local mall, where she spent several hours shopping for clothes, makeup and accessories. If Reese Bainbridge thought the outfit she had on last night was sexy, wait until he saw her in the things she bought today.

Pam knew how to dress to bring out her best assets, and dressed accordingly in every situation, but since Tom's accident she'd had to limit her spending, especially on clothes, so her wardrobe wasn't what she'd like it to be. But she'd remedied that situation today.

She groaned when she thought about how much money she'd spent. A big chunk of what she'd been able to save was blown. But it'd be worth it when she saw the reaction on Reese's face. At least, that's what she told herself.

She made it home and to her room without having to face anyone. Good. After a long, relaxing bubble bath, she took her time dressing.

Her surprise would be two-fold tonight. She wasn't usually here for the dinners that were served at seven o'clock sharp each night, since she was normally working. And when she *was* here, she didn't usually show up looking like a walking fashion show.

She didn't even know if Reese would be at home for dinner tonight, but if her plan was going to work she had to dress every night as if he would be here. Even if he didn't show for dinner, he'd be home sometimes in the evening, and she'd make sure he saw her whenever he did show up.

Smiling with satisfaction, she took one last look in the mirror. The mint green, three-piece pantsuit emphasized her green eyes. The material was soft and flowing, and she loved the way the duster-length jacket flowed around her when she moved. The bodice, while not too snug, fit well enough to accentuate her curves.

Feeling like a million dollars, Pam headed for the library, where Fiona liked for everyone to meet before dinner. She heard voices just before she reached the door of the library, and realized that Fiona and Reese were already there. They didn't see her approach, and she caught enough of the conversation to sense they were having a heated argument, and that part of it was about her.

"Should I come back after you're finished with this discussion?" she asked.

Startled, both people whirled to confront her. She watched with great satisfaction as two mouths dropped in astonishment.

"Pam, what are you doing here?" Fiona shot at her. "Why aren't you at work?"

"Oh, I got tired of working all the time," Pam said, holding Reese's gaze, but trying not to show the belligerence she felt. "I decided to quit the cleaning job. I gave my notice to them this morning." She thought she saw a brief moment of uncertainty flash in Reese's eyes, but it was gone before she could be sure.

"So, you'll be with us each night for dinner? Or are you going out? You look absolutely stunning!" Fiona came toward Pam to give her a closer scrutiny.

"Thank you, Fiona, and no, I'm not going out. I'll be joining the family for dinner."

"If you're not going out, why the hell are you dressed like that?" Reese's low voice sliced across the room from where he still stood. He wore a pair of black slacks and a tan knit pullover shirt.

Even though Fiona stressed that no one came to the table in attire that was too casual, she didn't require formal dress, either.

"Oh, I've decided that if I'm going to live in a beautiful house like this, I need to dress the part. Especially at dinner," Pam answered sweetly.

Fiona's face suddenly lit with glee. "You go, girl," she barely whispered for Pam's ears only.

Tom's arrival stopped any reply Reese may have been planning.

"Pam?" Tom's voice reflected the shock on his face.

"Hi, Tom, did you have a good day?" She greeted her brother warmly as she went to him and placed a kiss on his cheek, as she always did when she saw him at the end of their day.

"Why aren't you at work?" he asked, taking in her new look and about to comment on her clothes when Reese's voice suddenly interrupted them.

"She *says* she quit her cleaning job." Pam didn't miss the doubt he deliberately interjected.

"Oh, Pam, I'm so glad. I've been worried about you." Tom's sincerity touched Pam.

"Now that we have the family reunion over, can we possibly go in to dinner?" Reese interrupted.

"Reese, is it impossible for you to be civil?" Fiona impatiently asked him.

"If and when I find myself in a situation that deserves it, I can be extremely civil," came his sardonic reply as he led the way from the room.

"So you quit your cleaning job?" Reese's voice suddenly brought everyone's attention back to Pam.

Suzy had just finished bringing in the food, and everyone was beginning to eat.

"Yes," Pam answered, smiling sweetly at him as she cut into her baked chicken. She could tell that not knowing what concerning the cleaning job was really eating at Reese. But if he found out anything differently, he'd find it out from someone else.

"I see. Well, I wondered how long it'd be before you'd start taking advantage of the situation that you think you have here. Now I wonder how long it'll be before you quit your other job."

"Reese!" Fiona warned.

"That's okay, Fiona," Pam stopped her, before turning to fasten Reese with an icy green stare.

"Mr. Winger informed me today that I wouldn't be allowed to leave Winger & Thomas even if I wanted to. He said I am much too valuable for them to lose."

"And you're as confident about that as you are about your situation here, aren't you?" His taunting voice suddenly ignited the anger Pam had tried to conceal all evening.

"Oh, I'm sure some *imbecile* could come along and buy them out and cause me to lose my job, but I don't know of anyone desperate enough to do that right now. Do you, Reese?" Well, great! She'd said too much. Now he knew. She could tell by the blue gleam that engulfed her, that he knew.

"What do you mean, 'desperate,' Pam? Aren't you giving yourself way too much credit?"

"Will one of you please tell me what you're talking about?" Fiona suddenly interrupted the fiery exchange between the two.

"It's nothing!" Pam and Reese exclaimed in unison.

"Pardon me, Reese?" Suzy hesitantly interrupted. "Odis is on the phone. He says no one's showed up to clean the Winger & Thomas building, so what should he do?"

Pam almost choked on the bite of food she'd just put into her mouth, as laughter exploded from her. Reese gave her a scalding glare as he left the room to talk on the phone.

"Pam, I would really like to know what's going on," Fiona said. The look on her face implied that she intended to have an answer.

"Then you need to speak with your grandson, Fiona. Because the only thing I know is that Mr. Winger told me this morning that the security service was going to provide free cleaning for the building, and I wouldn't be needed anymore."

"What? Free? Why?"

"Pam—it seems that I need your help," Reese interrupted from the doorway. His face looked like a thunderstorm about to explode.

"Not tonight, Reese, I have a headache," Pam smiled sweetly.

"Damn it, Pam, Jen's baby got sick and she can't do the cleaning. I really need your help." For once, Reese Bainbridge was actually asking, not demanding.

"Know this, Reese. I'll go do the cleaning tonight, but it's for Winger & Thomas, not for you. I don't want to have to work in a dirty office tomorrow. I'll have to go change to work clothes."

"Well, at least finish your dinner," Fiona advised.

"I'm not in the mood for food right now," Pam said. "Maybe a little blood," she ground at Reese, "but not food."

"Reese, I will speak with you in my office right now," Fiona demanded, rising from her chair.

"Fifi—"

"NOW!"

Tom reached out and squeezed Pam's hand as she walked past him. "I want to talk with you as soon as we get a chance," he said.

Pam nodded and went to her room to slip into a pair of faded jeans and a worn T-shirt. The anger she'd fought all day was almost ready to pour out in the form of tears, but she fought them back. Okay, maybe tonight hadn't gone off without a hitch, but this was just the first night of the plan. She wasn't daunted yet.

Keys in hand, she was reaching for her car door when a voice startled her.

"We'll go in my car." Reese had been waiting beside her car.

"We?"

"Yes, we. I'm going to help you."

Pam couldn't stop the laugh that slipped from her throat. "The mighty Reese Bainbridge is going to clean toilets?"

"Just come on," he said, and headed for his car.

Reluctantly, Pam followed. She had no desire to be trapped in his small sports car with Reese Bainbridge. Such close quarters. Suddenly the reluctance left her as she realized she'd been handed a wonderful opportunity to follow through with part of her plan.

"It's really nice of you to help me like this," she said sweetly, as she slid into the seat beside him.

Reese glanced at her, sensing her change of attitude, but didn't respond.

After fastening her seat belt, which emphasized her breasts by slicing right between them, Pam stretched around to look into the back seat of the car. As she did, one of her breasts grazed Reese's arm as he was in the process of shifting gears. The gears ground as his arm momentarily froze at what he felt.

"Stop it, Pam!" he demanded.

"Stop what?" she asked innocently. She really hadn't planned what happened, but was encouraged by his reaction.

"I've already warned you, you don't want to play with me."

"Yeah, yeah, fire burns, blah, blah, blah," she taunted.

Before she knew what was happening the car had screeched to a stop and Reese was reaching for her. Her gasp of surprise gave him full access to her parted lips as his mouth covered hers.

He had stopped the car in the shadows of the trees that lined the long driveway to Bainbridge Hall, so they were in no danger of being seen. For that reason the swiftly approaching car was practically upon them before they were aware of the bright lights flooding them. Reese barely had time to sit back in his seat before the car came to a screeching stop beside them.

"Hi, Reese, darling, it's so good to see you," Sharon's voice called as she let her car window down. At that moment she spotted Pam, and her welcoming smile froze on her lips. "Am I interrupting something?" Her warm voice turned cold and hard.

"No, I just pulled over to check something," Reese evaded.

"Well, where are you going? Did you forget our date?" Honey dripped from her voice as she asked the question.

"Oh, damn! Actually, I did. I had an emergency arise at the Winger & Thomas building, and that's where we were headed. I'm sorry, Sharon, can we postpone until tomorrow night?"

"But, Reese," the honey voice suddenly turned to little-girl whining, "I'm all dressed up just for you."

"Oh, good grief! Just go!" Pam quietly admonished Reese. "I'm quite capable of taking care of the *emergency.*"

Not missing the sarcasm in her voice, Reese turned to Pam. "Are you sure?"

The green glare she sent him was all the answer he received.

"Okay, Sharon. Pam says she can handle the emergency. Meet us back at the house."

"Oh, that's wonderful!" Sharon gushed. "See, the fat girls are always easy-going and agreeable." She screeched her tires toward Bainbridge Hall.

Stunned, Pam couldn't believe what she'd just heard. Reese was busy negotiating a u-turn, but when he had the car headed back, he said, "Pam, don't pay any attention to Sharon, she's a spoiled brat."

"Easy going? Agreeable?" Pam choked. "I'll show that emaciated bitch what agreeable is!"

"Now, Pam—"

"Oh, don't 'now Pam' me, Reese. And if this is who you want to spend time with, then you don't need to be defending her actions to me. You just go have a wonderful time with her. After all, 'she got all dressed up just for you.'" Pam mimicked Sharon's little-girl voice.

As the car stopped, Pam got out and was about to let Sharon know just how disagreeable she could be, but Sharon had already wrapped Reese up in a welcoming hug. More like a seduction scene, Pam thought resentfully, as she headed for her car. But this wasn't the end of it. She *would* let Sharon know that she couldn't talk to, or about, her like that.

As she drove by them, Reese was helping Sharon into the seat that was still warm from where Pam had just been. *Jerk,* she mentally called to Reese as she sped past them.

Chapter 5

Pam almost stumbled with tiredness as she unlocked the door to Bainbridge Hall. It was past midnight and she assumed everyone would be asleep. She leaned wearily against the door and closed her eyes just for a moment. She wondered if she had the strength to make it up the stairs to her bed. Working, shopping, *and* cleaning had really taken it out of her. What a day!

Damn if she doesn't look sexier in jeans and a T-shirt than in those new clothes she bought, Reese thought resentfully as he watched her from the shadows of the library. Should he go to her and apologize for this evening? The male part of him that was stirring in his lower body wanted him to go to her and take her in his arms and hold her—well, maybe hold her for a moment, then move on to other things. But his rational brain rebelled against that. She was, after all, still the enemy.

So he watched her drag herself up the stairs and disappear into her room.

Tonight had been a joke. Sharon was even more immature than he remembered. Over the last couple of years he'd deliberately let her believe they were more of an item than they were. He needed someone around Fiona who'd keep him informed of any crazy actions she might come up with. His conscience bothered him a little at times for using Sharon, but he'd always convinced himself that it was just business, so it was okay.

But tonight she'd gotten on his nerves to the point that he didn't know how much longer he could take her. He might have to find some other way of keeping tabs on Fifi.

He had more of an interest in Bainbridge Corporation than he could let his grandmother know about. After all, his dad and grandfather had driven themselves to early deaths just trying to keep the company running, and even though he didn't plan on doing the same thing, he felt a certain amount of loyalty to them and their hard work. But if Fiona ever found out that he had one moment of concern about the company, she'd hound him until she had him buried in the running of it.

No. His entire being rebelled against that thought. He'd just have to find a way to let Sharon know he wasn't interested in her sexually, but still keep her loyal to him as a friend. Would that be possible?

The alarm persisted, pulling Pam's muzzy brain into reality. In slow motion she reached a weary hand out to try and stop the offending clock, only to knock it off the bedside table, where it rolled under the bed to continue its shrill sound.

"Well, this is just lovely!" she grumbled as she groggily rolled off the tall antique bed, landing on her hands and knees. She groped around under the bed but couldn't reach the screeching noisemaker. Since it was a wind-up clock she knew the alarm would run down, but she'd have to have it in the morning, so she might as well just crawl under the bed and get it right now, her still half-asleep brain reasoned.

Pam could barely squeeze under the bed. But, determined, she lay flat on her stomach and slid toward the hateful, still shrieking clock. Finally she captured the clock and snapped off the alarm. But as she tried to slide back from under the bed, she realized that the slight lifting that she had to do with her body in order to back up made her body too high and her rear end was catching on the bed. She couldn't get out.

Oh, hell! She was stuck! Sudden panic attack brought her fully awake. *Go forward*, her rational voice whispered. Belly-crawling forward, Pam's head and shoulders were out from under the bed when she was suddenly overcome with giggles over the situation. In spite of her uncontrolled laughing, she became aware of a loud pounding on the door.

"Pam!" Reese's concerned voice called. "Are you okay? I heard your alarm going on forever!"

She heard him, but the fact that Reese Bainbridge was standing outside her door and she was sprawled halfway out from under her bed just made the giggles worse. She was laughing so hard she lost her breath and could only make a wheezing sound when she tried to suck in air. Even though the doors to the house were thick, Reese was able to hear the noise she made. With growing concern, he burst

Pat Ballard

through the door to find her halfway out from under the bed, her head resting on her arms and her entire body shaking.

"What the hell?" he exclaimed and raced to her.

Looking up to see Reese hovering over her only made Pam laugh harder, as she held the clock up for him to see. As if just showing him the clock would explain the reason she was lying halfway under her bed.

But Reese didn't see the humor in the situation. He grasped her arms and roughly dragged her out from under the bed, helping her to a sitting position on the side of it.

The laughter died on her lips as she realized she sat in front of Reese Bainbridge with nothing on except her panties. She'd been too tired the night before to even put on her nightgown.

"Beautiful!" she heard his roughened voice whisper, as he reached out and gently cupped a breast in his hand.

Too overcome with emotion to respond, she watched in fascination as he leaned over and placed a soft kiss on the treasure in his hand before raising his lips to hers and claiming them completely as he pressed her gently back on the bed. As his lips explored hers, his hand worked magic on his newly found wonder, before starting to slowly work its way down Pam's body, seeking other pleasures.

Every fiber, every blood cell, every particle of Pam's very being was responding to this man. She had never been consumed with this kind of heat. Had never, in her wildest fantasies, thought that making love could feel like this. She wanted him to take her right now, right here, and the movements of her body were relaying that message to him.

The scream from the doorway that Reese had left open in his rush to get to her rudely snatched them back from their brief glimpse of

64

ecstasy, making them acutely aware of Fiona and Sharon gaping at them.

"Sharon dropped in to have coffee with you before she goes to work, Reese," Fiona stated, with a trace of triumph in her voice. The blue gleam in her eyes was almost blinding as she turned and walked away, leaving the open-mouthed Sharon rooted to the spot.

"Reese?" The little-girl whine skirted down Pam's spine like fingernails on a blackboard.

"Could you excuse us, Sharon?" Pam asked, as she stood up from the bed, allowing the gaping woman full view of her naked upper body. "I've got to dress for work, and Reese was just helping me wake up."

"Oh!" Sharon exclaimed indignantly. She turned and fled down the hallway.

"Serves her right, for that fat girl remark she made last night," Pam said, as she escaped quickly to her bathroom, leaving an astonished Reese staring after her.

He desperately wanted to follow her and finish what they'd started, but he knew he had to go to Sharon and calm her down. But what kind of an excuse was he going to give her for the position she'd caught them in? He had to think of something fast, or he'd lose his inside snitch, and wouldn't be able to keep up with Fifi's activities.

As the hot water poured over Pam's body, she started to relax a little. Well, one thing was for sure. She didn't have to wonder if Reese found her attractive or not. His actions of a few moments ago eliminated any doubts of that. But that still didn't mean he'd accepted her arrangement with Fiona. In fact, he'd probably be more adamantly against her than ever.

That suspicion proved to be very evident when Pam entered the library that night. As she made her entrance in black slacks with a hot pink silk oversized shirt that still managed to cling to and emphasize her curves, the first person her eyes fell upon was Sharon, clinging possessively to Reese's arm.

"There you are!" Fiona exclaimed, obviously relieved to see Pam.

Pam went straight to Tom and gave him a warm kiss on the cheek. "Hi, bro, how're you feeling today?" she asked. Then on impulse, she went to Fiona and gave her a light peck on the cheek. "And how are you tonight, Fiona?" she asked in the same warm voice.

"Can we go to dinner now that Miss Kissy Kiss has arrived?" Reese's voice was sharp with disdain.

"Now, Reese, don't be jealous, you had yours this morning," Pam oozed sweetly, looking directly at Sharon.

"What?" Tom's voice cracked, but was lost in Fiona's familiar cackle.

"Dinner's ready," Suzy called from the doorway.

As soon as the meal was over, Reese and Sharon left to "go out," as Sharon announced, giving Pam a triumphant smile. Later, in Tom's room, Pam's brother turned his wheelchair to squarely face her.

"Okay. What's going on? Am I to understand that Reese Bainbridge kissed you? Or you kissed him? Pam, what are you playing at?" Real alarm sounded in Tom's voice.

"Just calm down, Tom. Nothing is going on between Reese and me. Trust me, he still hates us being here as much as he ever did."

"Well, his not liking us being here has nothing to do with him responding to you as a beautiful woman, Pam. And I don't want you getting involved with him. You'll just get hurt!"

Pam placed a throw pillow in front and just to the side of Tom's wheelchair. Sitting down on it, she leaned her head against one of his legs. She missed the reassuring hugs Tom used to give her when he'd sense she had a problem. Now this was the closest thing she could get to a hug from him.

He reached out and stroked her hair. "Pam, talk to me. We don't talk much since we've moved here, and I miss that. Why were you and Reese kissing?"

Pam relayed the alarm clock story to Tom, and they were both in stitches from laughing at her ridiculous position under the bed.

"But how does Reese Bainbridge play into this?" Tom finally asked, wiping the tears from his face.

Pam had stopped her story just before the part where Reese had knocked on her door. She really didn't want to go into detail about the events that followed.

"Well, he heard me laughing and he came in and pulled me out from under the bed."

"And?" Tom persisted.

"Oh, nothing, really, it was just one of those moments when things kind of got out of hand."

"Pam, you're not telling me everything," Tom said, cupping his hand under her chin, raising her head to force her eyes to his.

"Big brother, you don't get to know everything that goes on in my life," she said, giving him her most charming smile.

"Just don't get hurt, okay?"

"You might need to be more worried about Reese," she said mysteriously, ignoring the little uneasy feeling that crept over her. "Now, tell me about your work," she changed the subject. "Are you still enjoying it? Is your back pain still staying subdued?"

"First, yes, the pain in my back is endurable most of the time. But I just can't figure out what Fiona is up to. She has me in her office a lot, going over things that I don't feel comfortable discussing with her."

"Why don't you feel comfortable?"

"Well, these are things that I don't feel like someone in my position should be privy to. I mean she's showing me some in-depth copies of the books, profits that are made and lost, and things like that."

"Maybe she just needs to share these things with someone who's interested in the company. You know she can't talk with Reese. Who else is there at Bainbridge Corporation that she can talk with? You know, someone on a personal level like you."

"Yeah, I guess so. But I still think it's kind of odd."

"Maybe she's grooming you to take over the company," Pam suggested.

"You'll always be a dreamer, won't you, little sister."

"Well, dreams do come true, you know. You just need to do a little dreaming of your own, big bro," Pam admonished, getting up and putting the throw pillow back on the small sofa.

"Leaving already?"

"Yes, I think I'll turn in early tonight, I'm kind of tired," she answered, heading for the door.

"Pam?"

"Yeah, bro?"

"Please be careful. I don't want you to wind up hurt from this situation. I couldn't stand it if you got hurt in the process of trying to fix my life."

Going back to Tom's chair, Pam leaned down and kissed his cheek. "I'm a big girl, remember? I can take care of myself, and I'm not going to get hurt."

As Pam made her way to the stairway to go to her room, she became aware of voices coming from the library, and looked in just in time to see Sharon's arms encircling Reese's neck as he lowered his lips to hers.

Wanting to escape before she was seen, she turned quickly and stumbled over a decorative spittoon that stood beside the library door. She managed to grab the doorjamb and not fall, but when she looked up, she was looking directly into Reese's surprised eyes.

"She's sneaking around, spying on us, Reese!" Sharon's accusing voice shattered the silence.

"In your dreams," Pam shot back at her. "I don't give a damn what you and Reese do!" And she turned and fled up the stairs to her room. She slammed the door hard enough that she was sure they heard if from the library. At least, she hoped they did.

She sat numbly on the side of her bed and stared at nothing. She realized she was sitting in the same spot where Reese had briefly made love to her this morning. Love? Ha! He'd groped her, that's what he'd done. And now he was down in the library kissing that airhead! Well, that just proved what kind of womanizer Reese Bainbridge was. But she'd known that, hadn't she? And she really couldn't care less about Reese and his women!

Then why did it hurt so much to see him kissing Sharon?

"No. No I won't even go there!" she said out loud, as she headed for the bathroom to take her shower.

But she spent a restless night, turning and tossing and trying to escape the image of Reese, kissing other women at times, then coming back to her and making her weak with his experienced touch.

Reese sat in the library for hours after he'd finally gotten rid of Sharon. Should he try and explain to Pam that he'd been giving Sharon a kiss of consolation, because he'd finally convinced her they could only be friends?

It really hadn't been that hard to convince her, after he offered to pay her for the extra work of "keeping an eye" on Fifi. He'd convinced her that his main concern was because Fifi was getting older and he was afraid for her health and mental well-being. He felt like a genuine jerk, but some things just had to be done, and this was one of them.

So, hopefully, Sharon would accept their arrangement and stop trying to seduce him every time they talked. Hopefully. She didn't do a thing for him in that area.

Pam, on the other hand, did a hell of a lot for him in that area. And he'd been about to lose control of himself this morning in her room. Thank goodness, Fifi and Sharon had interrupted them. All he needed was to get weak enough to make love to Pam.

Because he knew that once would never be enough. Especially after the way she'd responded to him this morning.

Or was she just faking it? Was that part of her game? To get him into the sack and get him besotted with her so she'd really have a toehold on his inheritance?

He kept forgetting that she was the enemy! He was really going to have to get a hold of his feelings for her. And that was going to be one of the hardest things he'd ever done.

No, he wouldn't explain anything to Pam. She didn't deserve an explanation. She was, after all, the enemy in his house.

Chapter 6

Fiona Bainbridge stood and gazed out of her office window at the black thundercloud looming over the Dallas skyline. Slowly approaching, like her own personal storm. She felt a little knot of panic as she stared out the window.

Time was such an enemy sometimes. And time was running out. She had to hurry if her plan was going to come together. And it *would* come together. She would see that it did, no matter how much time it took.

The knock on her office door brought her out of her reverie.

"Come in," she called, and watched as Tom Spencer carefully maneuvered his wheelchair into her office, careful not to bump the fine woodwork that surrounded the door.

Tom was such a good man. How had anyone allowed a company do to him what hers had done? Negligence. Pure and simple. Well, she was about to right that wrong.

"How are you this morning, Tom?"

"I'm fine, Fiona, and you?"

"Tom, I've made arrangements for you to have your back surgery next week," Fiona said, not answering his question.

"But Fiona, I told you I needed time to save money for the extra expenses the insurance won't cover," Tom reasoned. "And I don't have that yet."

"Consider all costs covered," Fiona said, finality in her voice.

"Why are you doing this?" Tom asked.

"I think I had forgotten, if I ever knew, how honorable some people can be. You and Pamela have reminded me of what honor is. I like you and Pam a lot. I'm finding out that you have a fine business mind. And that sister of yours," here a smile spread across her wrinkled face, "that sister of yours just tickles the hell out of me!"

"Pam is a one-of-a-kind person, I can tell you that," Tom agreed, love for his sister filling his voice with emotion. "But what has this got to do with you paying for all the expenses of my back surgery?"

"Tom, my company screwed you. And I mean big time! And now that I know what good people you and Pam are, that bothers me. It bothers me a lot! I'm not going to stop until you are back on your feet, living a normal life again. That's the least I can do for all that Bainbridge Corporation has put you and Pam through."

"But, Fiona—"

"No! No arguments, Tom. You should know me well enough by now to know that when I make up my mind, it's made up."

"You and my sister have a lot in common in the stubbornness area," Tom agreed, smiling broadly at Fiona.

"That's probably why I like her so much," Fiona replied, and then continued. "The doctors want to run some tests on you tomorrow, so you'll need to be at Baylor Medical Center at six o'clock. If you need to leave work and make any kind of arrangements today, then go."

"Will I be in the hospital overnight?"

"No, the tests should be done in one day, but if necessary, Pam and I can always bring you some pajamas to sleep in."

"Fiona, I—"

"Go Tom, I've got work to do." Fiona waved him off, not wanting to hear his thanks. This is one debt she would be glad to get settled before it was too late.

"For real?" Pam squealed, almost falling on top of Tom in her haste to hug him at his good news. "Oh, Tom—" Her voice choked up as tears poured down her face. Finally! Her beloved brother would have his life back!

They were in the library, waiting for the others to meet for dinner. "Okay, bro," she said, regaining her composure, "You can thank me properly when you're back on your feet!"

"And how is that?"

"Oh, I think first, down on your knees bowing and scraping, and apologizing for giving me such a hard time for filling out that application for Fiona's money. Yeah, that would be a starter." She nodded her head in satisfaction.

"Pamela Spencer, do I hear an 'I told you so' tone in your voice?" Tom's teasing note brought tears back to Pam's eyes.

"Oh, I'm sure your sister feels very satisfied with her accomplishments," Reese's voice shot at them from the doorway of the library, where he'd overheard the entire conversation. "But maybe after this surgery's over, you two can get out of my house." He continued into the library.

Pam was shocked at the contempt in his voice. Was it only yesterday morning that he'd held her and kissed her until she was melting onto the sheets of her bed?

"Yes, Reese," Tom's voice was calm and controlled. "I'm sure that as soon as this surgery is over, you'll be rid of us for good. I'm truly sorry we've been such a bother to you."

"Oh, I wouldn't count on that, at all," Fiona's voice interjected as she breezed into the room. "Reese, do I need to remind you again that this is my house for as long as I live? And that *I* say who is and isn't welcome here, for however long that is? And as far as I'm concerned, Tom and Pam can live here until the day that I die! Hell, they make things interesting around here. I never know when you're going to get a wild hair and take off to God only knows where, and leave me rattling around this huge house by myself. Well, I want them here, so that the next time you leave, I won't be alone."

"Maybe I don't plan to go away anymore, Fifi. Have you thought of that?" Reese could see that his grandmother was upset about something tonight, and he hadn't meant to add to her discomfiture.

"You plan on settling down, Reese?" Disbelief was evident in Fiona's voice. "Well, then you might as well make peace with the Spencers so we can all live here together in harmony."

"Dinner's ready," Suzy announced from the doorway.

"Whose money did you spend on all those new clothes?" Reese's voice caught Pam off guard, bringing her eyes to his piercing blue stare, which instantly lowered to the slight cleavage showing from the royal blue gauze top she wore with an off-white twill pantsuit.

Dinner was almost finished, and it was the first time Reese had addressed her during the entire meal.

"Reese!" Fiona scolded.

"It's okay, Fiona," Pam said, smiling at the astonished woman. "I'm used to his acerbic attitude by now. I think this is just his way of telling me he loves me," she cooed.

"In your dreams," Reese ground out, but his eyes were hot with memories, and belied the denial in his voice.

"And yours," Pam countered, holding his stare.

"Tom, I need for you to come to my office and get some papers to take with you in the morning," Fiona said, rising from her chair.

"I'll come too, since I'll be taking him to the hospital tomorrow," Pam offered, also getting up.

"Actually, Pam, I want to take Tom, because I want to make very sure that the doctors know exactly what I have in mind," Fiona said. "You and Reese go on to the library and we'll join you when we're finished."

"The queen has spoken," Reese sighed, watching Fiona and Tom leave the room.

"It's too bad you don't show your allegiance to the queen more often," Pam said, as she brushed past Reese, heading for the stairway.

"Where are you going?" he asked, catching up with her.

"To my room."

"No, you're coming to the library, to await the return of your pampered brother and my loony grandmother," he said, taking Pam's arm and leading her to the library.

Pam snatched her arm from Reese's tight grip, and in the process managed to whack him on the jaw with the back of her hand. Startled, they both stopped dead in their tracks and looked at each other, surprise registering on both their faces.

"Oh, Reese! I'm so sorry. I didn't do that on purpose," Pam said, reaching up and placing her hands on each side of his face.

Suddenly the intensity of the situation slammed into both of them.

"Prove it," Reese huskily whispered.

So, standing on tiptoes, Pam placed a soft kiss on the spot where her hand had struck his jaw. And then, remembering how his lips felt on hers, she placed feather kisses on each corner of his mouth until, with a groan, his wonderful mouth claimed her lips as he crushed her to his chest.

Neither of them was aware of how they wound up on one of the leather sofas. The only thing Pam was aware of was Reese's mouth devouring hers, driving her crazy, slowly tracing her lips with his tongue, then unhurriedly slicing it into her mouth to playfully fence with her own.

She was once again succumbing to the magic he seemed to enchant her with. She longed to lose herself in the total pleasure she knew he could bring her. Pleasures she knew she'd never experienced.

Suddenly her head was jerked rudely backwards, and a shrill voice was piercing her ears.

"So that's it!" Sharon screeched, holding on to her handful of Pam's hair. "It *is* the fat girl that turned your head. I knew something was wrong last night when you said you just wanted to be friends with me!"

"Sharon, let her go!" Reese's voice was low and threatening.

But Pam, not being one to remain too long in an inconvenienced situation, suddenly yanked her head, causing Sharon to lose her grip. Then, bounding off the couch, Pam grabbed a handful of Sharon's hair.

"How does it feel, bitch," she ground out, just as she realized she was holding a wig in her hand and Sharon was clutching her own mussed hair, trying to hide the hideous mess. Flinging the wig back at the horrified woman, Pam broke into peals of laughter, and realized Reese was also bent over shaking with laughter.

Slamming the wig on at an unnatural angle, Sharon fled the house with tears streaming down her face.

The two women sitting quietly talking in the hushed atmosphere of the hospital waiting room didn't pay any attention to the soft swoosh of the elevator doors slicing open, or to Reese as he stepped from the elevator.

He had never seen Fiona take to anyone like she'd taken to Pamela Spencer. It didn't make any sense to Reese. Of course, he knew why *he* took to Pam like he did, but Fiona? As far as he knew she'd never had any close personal friends. Just the required social acquaintances, but that's all. So why Pam? Or was this just an act to make him crazy? A way to try and force him to become involved in Bainbridge Corporation? Well, she could jolly well forget it!

"How's it going?" he projected his question ahead of him as he approached them.

"Reese? What are you doing here?" Fiona asked, truly surprised he'd show up for Tom's surgery.

"Why wouldn't I be here?" he asked, penning Pam with a blue-laser glance. "This involves my life too, doesn't it?"

"Now, Reese, if you've come here to cause disruption, just go away," Fiona ordered. "Pam is worried sick about her brother's surgery, and she doesn't need your foul attitude upsetting her more than she already is."

For the first time since he'd arrived Reese actually looked at Pam, and could tell that her eyes were red-rimmed, as if she'd been crying. He hated the knot of compassion that slammed into his guts, making him want to take her in his arms and tell her that her brother was going to be fine. She was the enemy, damn it! And he had to remind himself of that more and more often, lately.

Just then the doctor came into the room, and Fiona and Pam stood to hear what he had to say.

"Ms. Bainbridge, Pam, Tom has come through the surgery with flying colors. I'm convinced that after several months of physical therapy his back will be as good as new. He should be able to lead a very normal life."

Pam suddenly sat back into her chair, knees too weak to hold her up. It was over. Tom was going to have his life back. Tears flowed freely into her hands, which she had cupped over her face.

"Here, here, now, take it easy," a low, husky voice admonished, as she felt someone pushing a tissue into her one of her hands.

Through tear-blurred eyes Pam realized Reese had pulled up a chair and was sitting in front of her, trying to dry her tears. She was stunned at the open compassion she saw in his eyes momentarily, before he shielded the look with a more teasing one.

"The hard part's over now. You should be laughing, not crying!" he said, pulling her hands away from her face and holding both of them in one of his as he finished drying her tears with his other.

"Is that her husband?" the doctor quietly asked Fiona.

"Not yet," Fiona answered, just as quietly, taking in Reese's tenderness with sudden hope springing alive in her chest. She *knew* it! She'd known all along that he wouldn't be able to resist Pam, and if that look in his eyes right now told her anything, her plan might come together faster than she'd even dreamed!

Pam, remembering where they were and why, tore her eyes away from Reese's intent look and asked the doctor, "Can I see Tom now?"

"Not yet. He's in intensive care, and will be for several hours. He wouldn't know it if you were there," the doctor answered.

"But can I just peek in and see him for a moment?" Pam persisted.

"Okay, but just a moment," the doctor gave in. "By tonight, you should be able to say a few words to him."

When Pam returned to the waiting room, Reese was there alone. "Where's Fiona?" she asked.

"She said she had some work that couldn't wait, and that I was to take you to lunch," Reese answered.

"But don't you have things to do? I can just get a sandwich out of the vending machine here, and eat it while I wait."

"No. I was given strict instructions not to allow you to do that. I'm to take you somewhere nice and buy you a good, healthy lunch. The queen has spoken!" Some of the familiar, cynical Reese was creeping back into his voice, causing Pam to wonder if she'd only imagined the brief moment of gentleness she thought she'd seen earlier.

"But what if they need me?" she persisted.

"I gave my cell phone number to the doctor, and he promised to call immediately if he should need to contact you. So you don't have any excuses," he said, placing his arm gently around her shoulders and heading toward the elevator.

The sudden feeling of being shielded and protected that came from having Reese's arm around her shoulders rocked Pam to the core of her being. Surely it was only because she was feeling so vulnerable from Tom's surgery. She *must not allow* her feelings to get out of hand with Reese Bainbridge. She simply could not afford to fall in love with him.

As the elevator doors slid open and Reese followed her inside with his hand in the small of her back, a cold knot of fear gripped Pam's heart, for suddenly she knew that it was too late.

She was in love with Reese Bainbridge.

Chapter 7

Pam felt like a child again as she and Tom splashed around in the pool at
Bainbridge Hall. Swimming was part of his physical therapy. On rare
occasions, Pam was able to join him when he was doing his laps
around the pool. Today, he seemed to feel better than he'd felt since
before his accident. After spending several minutes in a fierce water-
splashing battle, they were hanging onto the side of the pool to rest
and catch their breath.

"You know we need to earnestly start looking for a place to live,"
Tom said, turning suddenly serious.

"I know," Pam answered, not really wanting to spoil the happy
mood with a serious discussion. But more than that, not wanting to
think about the time they'd have to leave Bainbridge Hall and the two
people she'd grown to love so deeply. She couldn't imagine not
having Fiona Bainbridge in her life on a daily basis. And Reese—well,

Reese was a different story. He'd avoided her as much as possible since the day of Tom's surgery. It was almost as if he'd sensed her revelation that she was in love with him, and tried to stay away from her.

"But?"

"But what?" she asked.

"I sense a 'but' in your answer."

"I just hate the thought of leaving this place, don't you? Have you grown to love it as much as I have?"

"Pam, you knew we couldn't stay here when we came," Tom scolded. "And you knew not to get too accustomed to these luxurious surroundings."

"I know. My head knows, but my heart won't listen," she said wistfully.

"Could your heart be longing for something other than the beautiful house and grounds?"

"Tom! What on earth are you talking about?" Pam tried to sound indignant.

"I've seen you looking at Reese, Pam. I'm so afraid you've fallen in love with him." Real worry etched Tom's voice.

"Oh, don't be ridiculous!" she chided. But she felt horrible for holding out on her beloved brother.

"You have, haven't you?" he persisted, seeing the pink that stained her cheeks.

"Oh, Tom—" Suddenly her eyes filled up with tears.

"No! NO!" Tom exploded. "I knew you were going to get hurt by this situation! My life is back on track, but you're going to have a broken heart! I hate this sacrifice you've made for me!"

"But it's not your fault that I'm stupid!" she shot back. "So don't go and try to lay the blame at your own door. I knew I was playing with fire. And I knew that I stood a real chance of getting hurt."

"But you can have it all. You don't have to leave Bainbridge Hall, *and* you can have Reese." Fiona's blue glare penned Pam to her chair.

"What are you talking about?" Pam asked. Fiona had called her to her office at Bainbridge Hall after they had finished eating dinner.

"I overheard you and Tom talking out by the pool this afternoon. I really didn't have any intention of eavesdropping on you, but I walked up just as Tom was questioning you about being in love with Reese. So I just decided to wait and hear the answer."

"Oh," was the only response Pam could utter. What was there to say if Fiona had heard her full confession of love for Reese?

"Pam, that first day that you came to see me, I said you were 'perfect.' Did you ever wonder what I was talking about?"

"Well, I later decided you meant because I'm not some tall, slim model-type, and you didn't think Reese would chase after me like he usually does other women. I assumed you thought it would be safe to have me in the house, because he would leave me alone." Pam had to fight to keep the resentment from her voice, and was surprised to hear the now beloved cackle erupt from Fiona.

"Exactly the opposite!" Fiona said.

"Excuse me?"

"I said you were perfect because I knew as soon as I saw you that Reese would have a hell of a hard time keeping his hands off of you!"

"I'm sorry, Fiona, but I'm totally lost here. What are you talking about?" True confusion clouded Pam's thinking power.

"Come here," Fiona said. Using a key from her key-chain, she opened the bottom drawer of her desk and pulled out a huge stack of old magazines. "Look at these and tell me what you see."

Pam's eyes grew large as she took in picture after picture of Marilyn Monroe at her largest size. And there were several magazines featuring Jane Mansfield. "It's obvious that I see magazines with pictures of Marilyn Monroe and Jane Mansfield. But why do you have them and why are you showing them to me?"

"They're Reese's," came the candid reply. At Pam's blank look, Fiona continued. "Don't you see what this means? Reese likes women with some flesh on them. And I knew as soon as I saw you that you'd be hard for him to resist."

"But Fiona, just because Reese collects memorabilia about these two women doesn't necessarily mean he likes the body type. It may just mean he knows these magazines and photos are a good investment," Pam reasoned. "And even if he does like this body type, he obviously doesn't like me because of what I represent."

"That's my point exactly. The boy doesn't have sense enough to figure out what's best for him, so you and I are going to have to do it!" Now a new gleam was in those amazing blue eyes.

"But Fiona—"

"Hush, girl, and listen to me. When my husband died, I promised him on his deathbed I would make sure someone in the family was running Bainbridge Corporation before I died. But little did either of us know that our only son would die so early, or how stubborn Reese was going to wind up being about all of this.

"And it's becoming more and more obvious that Reese is determined not to have anything to do with the company. And even if he got married and had a child, I'd be dead before that child got old enough to decide if he were going to be a part of Bainbridge Corporation or not. So I've got to act now! I've had a plan for some time now, and was patient to wait and let it happen. But time has turned on me, and I have to take measures to make that plan happen quickly. And you're going to help me. I know you will, because it'll be in the best interest for you and Tom if you do."

Pam was becoming frightened at the wild look that had crept into the older woman's eyes as she talked.

"Fiona—"

"Shhhhhhh! Now listen to me. Here's the plan. If you and Reese are married, then technically, Tom will kind of be in my family. Tom is a wonderfully gifted businessman. I've been showing him the books on Bainbridge Corporation, and he has a remarkable grasp of what's going on. He's the perfect person to turn the running of the company over to."

"But Reese doesn't love me, Fiona, and he would never ask me to marry him, so you'll have to come up with a different plan," Pam managed to interrupt long enough to make her point.

"There's not enough time for a different plan. This one *has* to work." Pam sensed the desperation in Fiona's voice, but before she could question her, Fiona continued. "I know Reese is attracted to you. Girl, I saw what he was doing to you on your bed that morning. And I saw him kissing you in the pool one day. So I know he has the hots for you! But I don't have time to wait for him to finally decide that you're the woman he wants to spend his life with. Even if he doesn't love you now, he'll learn to love you. You can *make* him love you. So here's the plan. You're going to get him drunk and marry him! Then I can make the will out to leave Bainbridge Corporation to Tom. Just think what you'll be doing for your brother! He'll be set with a multi-million dollar business! He'll never have to worry about finances again! And neither will you, because I plan to leave Reese set for life, even though he doesn't want my business." Was it sadness or bitterness that crept into her voice?

There were so many holes in this plan that Pam didn't know where to start to tell Fiona that none of this would work. And she was really becoming concerned at the crazed look in the older woman's eyes. Had Fiona gone off the deep end? She had to find a way to discourage her.

"Fiona, first, this isn't Las Vegas, this is Texas. I can't get Reese drunk and marry him the same day. There are licenses and blood tests that are necessary. And, besides that, I just can't do it."

"I'll take care of all of that. You just think about this and decide. But don't wait too long. As I said, time has suddenly become the enemy here. And just think of what you'll be doing for Tom. Now go. I have to get some rest." She waved Pam away from her.

Pam closed the door softly behind her. Fear engulfed her. Something was terribly wrong with Fiona. She was acting like a woman possessed. Pam had never seen her eyes flashing so blue. Had never seen that look of panic in them. Had never seen Fiona looking so small and frail as she did when Pam left her sitting in that huge room alone.

Pam turned and tossed all night, troubled by shadowy dreams and unanswered questions. She was relieved when the alarm went off. But her mind didn't become free of worry just because she was awake. She continued to worry about Fiona all day.

That night, when everyone met in the library, Pam wondered if Fiona really did look more drawn and pale than usual, or if she were just imagining it.

Reese, running late, burst into the room in a foul mood. Pam could tell as soon as she saw him that he was going to be a pain in the neck during dinner. And she was right. He picked at and found fault with everything everyone said, until finally Fiona grew tired of hearing him.

"Reese, why don't you just leave the room, if you're so unhappy with our company?" she suggested.

"Why can't these people just leave my house?" he countered, looking blue daggers at Tom before his eyes rested on Pam to glare at her.

"Because I don't want them to leave. And I thought we had this settled!" Fiona was becoming agitated.

"No, it won't be settled until they're out of here," he ground between clenched teeth.

"Pam and I are making plans to move as soon as we can find a place to live," Tom interjected, trying to halt the argument between Fiona and Reese.

"Like hell you are!" Fiona practically yelled. "You two aren't going anywhere as long as I'm alive and we have this huge house to rattle around in. There's no reason for you to pay rent or a house payment when this house is available."

"Well, that just about does it, as far as I'm concerned!" Reese bellowed, sliding his chair back from the table. "I'm out of here as soon as I can find another assignment. I won't stay in this house with these freeloaders. Fifi, I'm sorry you've chosen strangers over your own flesh and blood, but since you have, you enjoy them. I'll have Sharon call me when it's time to make the funeral arrangements!"

"REESE!" Three voices shouted at him at the same time, but he didn't slow down as he went through the door.

Pat Ballard

A stunned silence followed his departure. Pam couldn't believe what she had just heard. How dare he talk to his grandmother like that! Seeing the tears glistening in Fiona's awesome blue eyes was the last straw for Pam. That arrogant bastard needed to meet his match!

"Activate your plan, Fiona," Pam said, getting up to go in search of Reese to try and get him to apologize to his grandmother.

"What does that mean?" Tom asked.

"You'll know soon enough," Fiona cackled, as Pam left the room.

90

Chapter 8

Raw fear clutched Pam's throat and held on as the long limo pulled up in front of the MGM Grand Tower Hotel, a deluxe, sprawling, high-rise mega resort and casino located on the south end of the Strip at Tropicana Avenue in Las Vegas, Nevada.

How on earth had she allowed Fiona to talk her into this crazy scheme? It was *never* going to work! Reese would probably wind up putting them both away for being totally off their rockers. And he would be perfectly justified in whatever actions he did decide to take. But he deserved it. He'd been such a jerk lately. Even more so than he normally was.

"This way," her traveling companion directed, taking her arm to guide her through the throng of people who were in Vegas to have a wonderful time and enjoy their surroundings. Was she the only one here with an ulterior motive?

Tony—Fiona said that's the only name Pam needed to know—led her through the casino into a back room where the lights were dim. Two people sat at a table in a far corner, their heads close together. As Pam and Tony approached, one of the men looked up and Pam realized it was Reese. She could tell he was already drunk by the silly grin on his face.

"Pam? Ish that you? Wathehell you doing here?" he slurred.

"Hi, Reese. I came to be with you," she answered. At least that much was the truth.

"Well, get your shexy shelf over here and sit beshide me," he beckoned, sliding a chair close to him.

"Boysh, thish is the damndest sexiesht woman I've ever met in my life!"

"This may be easier than we'd planned," Tony murmured to the man sitting with Reese. Then as an afterthought, he introduced Pam. "Pam, this is Ronald. He's made sure that Reese, here, is very agreeable. Ronald, Pam."

Pam was sitting snugly tucked under Reese's arm now, and even though she knew he was drunk, her heart still felt like it was trying to push its way through her throat, just being this close to him. And he had called her sexy! Well—he'd tried to call her sexy. Is that what he really thought? Was the liquor allowing him to let his true feelings come out?

"Well, old boy," Tony said, clapping Reese on the shoulder. "If you think she's that sexy, why don't you just ask her to marry you? You're in Vegas, you know."

"You're right! Thass a good idea!" Reese exclaimed. "Baby, will you marry me? Right now? Tonight? That'll show Fifi who's in charge of my life!"

As the two men bent double laughing at their good fortune, Pam felt a terrible guilt wash over her. What was she about to do to Reese's life? And to her own? "Remember," Fiona had admonished, "You're doing this for Tom. And as a favor to me. And for Reese, too. I just want Reese's life to be happy before I leave this earth."

"Well, if you're going to get married, we'd better get on over to the court house and get the license, hadn't we?" Tony asked.

"Shure, less go," Reese agreed, trying to stand and pull Pam up with him at the same time.

Ronald took Reese's arm and helped him stand. Then the two men basically supported him through the crowd to the waiting limo.

Pam sat and watched Reese as he lay sprawled across the bed, sleeping the sleep that only a drunk can sleep.

After the rushed wedding, with Tony and Ronald standing in as witnesses, the two men had brought Reese up to this plush hotel room, helped him out of his pants and shirt, and assisted him in getting under the bed covers, as Reese was very close to passing out by then.

Cold chills crept up her spine just thinking of the hell she was going to catch when he woke up in the morning and found out they were married. Now, in the aftermath of the rush to get Fiona's plan carried out, deep, dark reality was setting in. She had tricked Reese Bainbridge into marrying her! Well, it'd been easier than any of them had expected, since he'd actually proposed to her. She'd thought she would be the one to have to do that. And at least she had witnesses to his proposal.

When she'd left Dallas this morning, there was no concrete plan on how she was supposed to get him to marry her. Fiona had just told her to figure it out as she went along. The basic plan was that Ronald would see to it that Reese was close to being drunk by the time she got there, and she'd have to decide what to do from there. Tony and Ronald would be there to help in any way they could, Fiona had tried to assure her.

Earlier in the week when Fiona had heard Reese talking on the phone, making plans to meet an old buddy in Vegas for the weekend, she'd seen her chance and jumped at it. Calling Pam into her office, she'd laid out all the details. She'd called in a favor that Tony owed her and convinced him to help with the plan.

What was Tom going to say? He'd been kept in the dark about all the plans, because both women knew he'd have vetoed it on the spot if he'd known what was going down.

Reaching for the phone, she dialed the number to Bainbridge Hall.

"Hello?" Fiona practically yelled into the phone.

"It's done," Pam said, trying to keep the weariness from her voice.

"Yes! I *love* it when a plan comes together! Where is he?"

"Asleep."

"Pam, don't ever regret going after what you want. Now, you make him love you, girl! You can do it!" And with that familiar cackle, Fiona hung up the phone.

Too weary to think about it any more, Pam curled up on top of the covers beside Reese, still fully dressed. Her intention was just to rest her eyes, but exhausted sleep claimed her as soon as her head touched the pillow.

Pam drifted slowly out of the deep sleep that had engulfed her. Her subconscious mind was telling her she really didn't want to wake up and face what was coming. But, as if being willed to open, the first thing her eyes fell on was the blue glare of the man facing her.

She didn't move. Didn't react at all. Just lay gazing back into the eyes that held her captive just as a snake charms and immobilizes its prey.

"I do have a few questions, if you're awake now," Reese's very soft, almost too soft, voice broke the silence.

"Okay," Pam barely whispered.

"First, why are you in Las Vegas? Second, why are you lying fully clothed in my bed? And third, are you protected against getting pregnant?"

"Pregnant?" Pam screeched, now fully awake.

"No, answer the first question first," Reese instructed, still not having moved a muscle.

"I'm in Las Vegas because Fiona wanted me to come be with you," she answered truthfully.

"And?"

"I'm fully dressed because I didn't have a place to stay, and I just slept in your bed," she lied.

"And?"

"Yes," she whispered again.

"Why don't I remember getting into bed? And why don't I remember you being here with me? Because if I'd known you were in my bed, you sure as hell wouldn't still be dressed!"

"You were already drunk when I got here. You were having drinks with Ronald."

"Who is Ronald?"

"The man you were having drinks with," Pam repeated, knowing she was sounding daft.

"I don't know a Ronald." Reese was beginning to grow weary with the word games. "And I don't *ever* get drunk. So did this Ronald put something in my drink to help me reach my inebriated state?"

"I don't know. As I said, you were already drunk when I got here."

"I'm tired of talking now. You've been wanting to get into my bed since day one, so now that you're here, I'm going to give you what you've been wanting!" He reached for Pam, but she scooted quickly backwards out of his reach.

"You really are a pompous asshole, aren't you?" she ground at him.

"What's the problem? You said you were protected against getting pregnant. You're here, and there's no one to interrupt us this time. Don't tell me you're a virgin? What? You're on the pill just to regulate your periods, right? But you're actually a virgin. I've heard that one before."

"No, Reese, I'm not a virgin. I was raped when I was 13 by an upstanding 18-year-old neighborhood boy. I became pregnant, but lost the baby. Ever since then, I've stayed on the pill just to be safe against guys who can't control their urges."

"I'm sorry that happened to you. But if you think that noble speech is going to stop me from making love to you, you're wrong. Now come here." He moved swiftly, catching Pam's wrist and pulling her back to him. And suddenly she was on her back, and he was towering over her, with both hands on each side of her head, his thumbs gently stroking the hair back from her face.

"Reese!"

"Pam?" Before she could answer, he was lowering his lips to hers. But he didn't cover her lips in the kiss she was expecting. Instead, he gently licked her lips before sucking her full bottom lip into his mouth and gently biting it before sucking on it again.

"You like that?" he whispered, ever so lightly licking her lips again. "Tell me you like it," he urged, now taking her top lip into his mouth and stroking it with his tongue. "Tell me, Pam. Say you like what I'm doing. Open your eyes and look at me, and tell me you want more."

Pam opened her eyes to be enveloped with the most tender look she'd ever seen on Reese Bainbridge's face. Surely he couldn't hate her, if he was looking at her like this. And remembering Fiona's words to make him love her, she knew that she would make love to him today, even if she didn't make him love her—yet.

"Yes, Reese," she sighed, "I like what you're doing."

"Do you want more?" he urged, again flicking his tongue across her mouth before gently easing it between her lips, and past her teeth, in a slow, rhythmic motion.

Pam's answer was a soft moan, giving Reese all the answer he needed. Inch by inch he undressed her, and inch by inch he kissed, caressed, and loved each spot of her body he uncovered. By the time he consummated their marriage, Pam knew she would never love another man the way she loved Reese Bainbridge. He entered her very soul when he entered her body, and she knew she'd been branded for life.

Pam stepped from the bathroom, fully dressed. She knew she had to tell Reese they were married, but she'd put it off until the last moment. The marriage license was tucked safely inside her purse, and if she didn't tell him, there was really no way of him knowing about it right away, was there? Did she have to destroy the surreal mood that his beautiful lovemaking had seemed to surround them with? Maybe she'd just wait until they got back to Bainbridge Hall, then let Fiona take part of the heat when Reese found out.

She saw that room service had delivered brunch and Reese was waiting for her. The table was spread with a wonderful array of food, and she realized she was very hungry, since she hadn't really eaten since leaving Dallas the day before.

"Come on and grab some of this wonderful food before it gets cold," Reese directed. "Although you look good enough to eat in that hot pink outfit. Maybe we'll just have to let the food get cold!"

"Reese! I'm hungry," Pam argued, while loving the new look of possession and familiarity in Reese's eyes.

"I am too, baby. I've been hungry every since the first time I saw you. And if I'd known what a live wire you are in bed, there's no way I could have waited this long to have you." By now he had his arms around her and was breathing his softly spoken words into her ear.

"But even as much as I want to love you again, right now I really do need to clear up some lingering questions about last night and how you came to be here with me. Your story doesn't hold water, you know, but earlier I wasn't in the mood to think about that. So why don't we talk while we eat, hmm?"

Pam's palms were suddenly coated with a thin film of perspiration, and her heart thudded against her chest. *Don't panic!* she admonished herself. *Just take a deep breath and stay cool.*

As hungry as she'd thought she was, she put only a few items on her plate and tried to go through the motion of eating, but her mouth was so dry everything just wadded up like cotton and she had to wash it down with water.

"So who is Ronald?"

"I don't know, Reese, I thought you knew him."

"Pam, please don't play me for a fool. Don't you think I know that your being here has something to do with one of Fiona's schemes? And I can't help but believe that this Ronald plays a big part in it. Now who is Ronald?" Although Reese's voice still held the tenderness that he'd shown since making love to her, there was a determination there now that let Pam know she would have to tell him the truth.

A loud, frantic pounding on the door saved her from having to answer right then. Casting a questioning look at Pam, Reese went to the door and opened it.

"Mr. Bainbridge, I'm Tony and this here's Ronald. I hate to interrupt you, but we have some bad news. Your grandmother is dead!"

Chapter 9

Tears slid unheeded down Pam's cheeks as she gazed at the casket that waited to be lowered into the ground. There were so many questions swirling in her head. Was Fiona really gone? Had she known all along that she was dying? What was going to happen now? How on earth was she going to explain the marriage to Reese without Fiona's help?

She glanced at Reese, who sat stone-faced and unapproachable, as he had remained since the news of Fiona's death. She'd tried on one occasion to talk to him about the marriage, but he'd brushed her off, saying he didn't have time to talk to her. So what had he been doing? She'd only seen him a couple of times since they'd returned from Vegas.

He didn't have to take care of the funeral arrangements. Fiona had everything planned, down to the last detail. She had been organized and in control even in death.

A kindly old minister was speaking comforting words to the few people who had come to the cemetery to show their last respects. And then it was over.

As the little group drifted away, the funeral attendants lowered the coffin that held Fiona's frail body into the gaping hole. Pam heard the dull thump as it settled into place at the same time she heard the groan rip from Reese's throat. She glanced up in time to see him, his back rigid, walking toward his waiting car.

Tom, who had sat stunned and quiet through the entire ordeal, took her hand. "Let's get out of here," he whispered.

Wanting to stay and say a last goodbye to Fiona, yet not wanting to watch that cold dirt pile up on top of her, Pam let Tom lead her to their car.

"Well, I guess this leaves us in the house-hunting position," Tom said, getting into the driver's seat. "And who knows what'll happen with my job! Just as I think I'm getting ahead again, the old gal snatches the rug out from under me!"

"Tom! I can't believe you're talking like that! You've been hanging around the Bainbridges too long. You're beginning to sound as cynical as one of them."

"I'm sorry, Pam. That was uncalled for. I'm just pissed that she died on me before I had a chance to pay her back for all she's done for us."

"Well, don't make any long term plans before the reading of the will this afternoon."

"What do you mean? Do you know something I don't?"

Should she tell him everything now? But what if Fiona had changed her mind? She didn't want to set Tom up with the wrong information. "No, I don't really know anything, I just think we should wait. We're to meet at six o'clock for the reading."

"And I think, little sister, that you're holding out on me."

Thankfully, they were pulling into the Bainbridge estate, so she didn't have to argue with him.

As the small group gathered in Fiona's office, Pam's breath came in short pants, and she was afraid she was going to hyperventilate if her tension grew any worse.

Dan Smythe, the family lawyer, sat at Fiona's desk and waited for everyone to be seated.

"First, I want to tell everyone the cause of Fiona's death. She had known for about a year and a half that she had a rare type of leukemia. She didn't want friends or family to know. She said people would assume she was a weaker person if they knew she was sick. The cancer was in remission until about a month ago, when it reoccurred with a vengeance, according to her doctor. In fact, he said she should have been gone weeks ago, but she seemed to be willing herself to live for some reason. And, as we're all saddened to know, she lost the battle a few nights ago. She just went to bed and didn't wake up. If it's any comfort, her doctor said she died with a smile on her face. Knowing Fiona, she'd probably just wrapped up a deal she was pleased with," he said with a chuckle.

Pam hardly heard his voice as he droned on about the legal ramifications of the will, and that Fiona's last wishes were unequivocally final.

"Anyone who wants to argue with Fiona's last desires can consider themselves completely out of the will," he admonished dogmatically. "And now the will."

"To Tom Spencer, I leave Bainbridge Corporation. The company shall remain his until his death, or until he is no longer capable of managing the property. He is to be in total charge of the running of the company. In my sound mind and judgment, I am convinced he is the only person I know who is capable of operating Bainbridge Corporation in the manner that my husband would have wanted it handled."

Pam heard Reese's quickly indrawn breath. She stole a glance at him to find him glaring at Tom.

"Spencer, I have to give it to you. I don't know how, but you managed to wrap her around your little finger!"

"Reese, as you know," the lawyer started reading again, *"I promised your grandfather on his deathbed that I would do all I could to leave the family business to a family member. Since you were so dead-set and determined not to be any part of Bainbridge Corporation, I did the next best thing. Tom Spencer is as close to being a part of the family as I could get. You'll understand when the next part of the will is read."*

Pam got the uncanny feeling that she heard a familiar cackle as the lawyer continued to read.

"To Reese and Pamela, Mr. and Mrs. Reese Bainbridge, I bequeath my remaining properties. These will be instated in full after you return from the honeymoon of your choice. But there must be a honeymoon!

"So you see, Reese, Tom is now your brother-in-law, and can be considered a family member."

Absolute silence engulfed the room. Pam kept her eyes glued to the lawyer, afraid to look in any direction.

"Dan, could you please read that last part again?" Reese's voice was dangerously quiet.

Pam had handed over the marriage license to Dan as soon as they'd returned from Las Vegas. She'd wanted to see if it were really binding and legal, and he'd assured her that it was.

"Reese," Dan calmly addressed him, "Fiona was only doing what she thought was best—"

"Read-the-last-section-again!" Reese ground out between clenched teeth.

Dan read the section again.

"You conniving bitch!" he said, standing abruptly and sending a blue glare at Pam. "There'll be a honeymoon, all right! We fly out of Dallas in the morning at six o'clock. I'm on assignment to finish a project in the Appalachian Mountains. But I'd pack something a little sturdier than those flimsy things you've been wearing around here, trying to temp me with. They won't be too practical climbing around on the mountains!"

The door slammed loudly as he left the room.

"Pam, what have you done?" They were back in Tom's room, and he had turned on her as soon as the door closed.

"It seems that I have sealed our future!" She tried to make light of the situation, even though her insides were heavy with unknowns.

"Don't!" She'd never heard this note in Tom's voice. "Don't even try and make light of this horrible thing that you've done!"

"But, Tom—"

"No! Pam, no." His voice cracked as tears finally spilled over and rolled down his cheeks. "You've sacrificed your own life to give me back mine. That's a price that's too high to pay. And there's nothing I can do to save you from what you've done, is there? I can't save you from that jerk! What on God's green earth were you and Fiona thinking about? What?" He didn't even try to hide the look of horror on his face.

"Tom, I'm in love with the jerk," Pam's quiet voice reminded her brother as she put her arms around him, trying to comfort him.

"So this is it? This is the way it has to be?" He sat down in the nearest chair.

"Yes, I'm afraid it is."

"But we can have the marriage annulled! Forget the will! I don't give a damn if we cause Reese Bainbridge to lose everything. We don't have to go through with this." Again he was on his feet, as if he had solved the problem.

"We've consummated the marriage." Pam couldn't bear to look into her brother's eyes as she revealed her latest secret.

"Oh, Pam. God help us! You've sold your soul to the devil!"

Chapter 10

"Just put those packs down anywhere," Reese directed the guide who'd helped carry the backpacks and bundles up the winding trail that seemed to lead them at least a mile up the steep mountain.

The guide gladly dumped his heavy load on the ground, accepted Reese's tip, and made his way back down the mountain.

"Welcome to your honeymoon, Darlin'." Sarcasm laced his voice as he spoke to Pam for the first time since they'd left Dallas early this morning. She was astonished at the cold fury that seared her as his eyes met hers. Again, the first time he'd even looked her way the entire day.

"I hope you enjoy the luxurious surroundings. If you need anything, just ring for room service," he said with a nasty chuckle, and picked up what Pam assumed was his camera equipment and stalked off.

Pam glared angrily at his departing back, which was basically all she'd seen of him the entire day. They'd left Bainbridge Hall at six a.m. sharp and headed for the Dallas/Fort Worth International Airport, for what Pam thought would be a commercial flight. But after having to almost run to keep up with his ever-departing back, she was surprised—why she should be surprised was beyond her—to be led to a private Lear Jet with Bainbridge Corporation emblazoned in bold letters across its side. Upon boarding it, Reese had taken the pilot's seat and proceeded to fly them to the airport at Ashville, NC, where they'd gotten into a Jeep and headed for a small town called Cherokee. There, Reese had made arrangements for the guide who'd helped carry their camping equipment up the mountain, where she stood now, alone, with resentment growing in leaps and bounds, forming a huge caldron of burning bile in the pit of her stomach.

She sank slowly onto a big rock, glancing first to make sure no snakes or spiders lurked in the shadows. The camping spot Reese had chosen was a clearing that backed up to a sheer rock wall that seemed to go straight up. From all other sides, thick forest surrounded her. Songbirds were beginning to restart their chorus after having been interrupted by the human voices.

From the steep climb on the way up, she'd thought they had to be close to the top of the mountain, but looking up at the rock wall she knew they weren't even close to being at the top. This was just a flat outcropping on the side of the mountain.

Glancing back at the camping equipment, a smile tried to make its way through her tightly clenched lips. Ah, the things Reese Bainbridge didn't know about her! Like the fact that she probably knew more about camping than he did, having grown up with a father who was a faithful Boy Scout leader and a brother who had won every medal and badge of honor the Scouts had to offer. And that their summers, as a family, were spent traveling and camping in every out-of-the-way spot imaginable. "It'll teach you survival skills," her dad had said repeatedly.

So should she make herself useful and go ahead and set up camp? Or should she just let the self-satisfied Mr. Reese Bainbridge think she was totally miserable, like he intended her to be?

The smile grew larger as she made her decision. "I think I'll just play the helpless maiden for awhile," she said out loud. Her voice and the satisfied laugh that followed again hushed the songbirds to total stillness, allowing the sound of falling water to penetrate her thoughts.

Water? Water! The last stream she'd seen was far below at the bottom of the mountain. She hadn't even considered how they were going to bathe or cook. She was about to get up from the rock and try to find the source of water when she heard clumping in the thick undergrowth close to her.

Jumping up and moving quickly away from the brush thicket, her heart pounding painfully in her chest, she watched as Reese made his way out of the bushes.

"I'm sorry, ma'am, I didn't mean to frighten you," he said, turning quickly from her to put his camera equipment on the ground. But he didn't turn quickly enough to keep Pam from seeing the slight twitch of his lips, as if he were fighting a smile.

"You did that on purpose, Reese!" she accused, fury rising in her throat.

"I forgot to tell you that you need to be very careful in these woods. Bears still roam here."

Before she could do more than gasp at his words, he continued, "I guess we'd better get these tents set up, it'll be dark soon. And it will be very dark out here in these woods. No city lights to scare all the monsters away. No big fancy house to keep you warm and happy. No one to fix your meals like you were becoming accustomed to at Bainbridge Hall. Poor Pam, just as she thought she'd landed in the perfect spot, it all falls apart. You been sitting on that rock feeling sorry for yourself ever since I left?" All the time he talked, he'd been busy unpacking the camping equipment.

Great, Pam thought as she glared at him. All day he doesn't say a word, and now he won't shut up!

She sank back to the rock where she'd been sitting before. So many responses tumbled through her mind that she didn't know which one to hurl at him first. How dare he! What a jerk he was turning out to be! Even more of a jerk than she'd thought he was.

"If you don't mind, make yourself useful," his voice interrupted her angry mental ranting. "That's an air mattress," he said, tossing a bag to her. "Unless you want to sleep on the hard ground, you'd best start blowing that thing up."

She carefully took the folded, deflated mattress from the protective plastic bag it was in, hoping to find an air pump inside the bag. There wasn't one, so she proceeded to blow the mattress up with her mouth. Blowing up the mattress made good use of her pent up anger, and it was at the correct size in no time. She carefully placed the valve into the hole to keep the air from leaking back out before looking up to find Reese watching her. His eyes rested on her lips, which were now red and slightly swollen from blowing on the mattress. Just for a moment there was no anger in his eyes before he turned abruptly and went back to pitching the tents.

Two tents, Pam noted. A large one, and a smaller one. She supposed the smaller one was for the equipment. For the first time today she considered the sleeping arrangements. Oh, hell! She was going to have to share a tent with him. Oh, hell!

In what seemed to Pam like a very short time, Reese had both tents pitched. He then sat down on another rock, close to the one Pam had claimed, took out another air mattress and a portable air pump and proceeded to inflate a huge—twice the size of the one he'd given her—air mattress. His mattress was at least a queen size!

Horrified, she watched him use the air pump. To her amazement, he had the audacity to laugh.

"All you had to do was ask if we had a pump," he said when he'd finally gotten his breath from laughing. "But no! You, Pamela Spencer, are not going to stoop to ask for anything, are you? Why, that would be beneath you! But wait—I forgot. You did stoop to ask for something, didn't you? You asked for Fiona Bainbridge's estate! You not only asked for it, you got it! But you wouldn't ask for an air pump." He shook his head as if he just couldn't understand it.

Pam had had enough. She was tired, she was hungry, she was totally frustrated, and she felt very close to tears. How could she ever have thought she loved this person, she asked herself, glowering at him all the while.

"Reese," she chose her words very carefully, keeping her voice calm, "if you're quite finished, I think I'll call it a day." She picked up her mattress and claimed the small tent. Let him sleep with his damned equipment, she thought resentfully, as she threw her mattress inside the tent and followed it in.

Miserably, she curled up on the mattress in the fetal position, with her back to Reese and any other harsh words he might have wanted to sling at her. She desperately wanted to cry, but sleep claimed her before she'd decided if that was a good thing to do or not.

Pam came slowly awake. She was aware of several things at once. She was miserably hot, she was in an uncomfortably cramped position, she was hungry, it was very dark, and her bladder was painfully full.

Great! Now she'd have to go out in the dark and try to find a place to relieve herself. If only she'd taken time to grab her pack before running away from Reese to hide in this tent. It had a flashlight in it. In fact, it had almost anything she could need for a short period of time.

Suzy had been wonderful last night in helping Pam pack for her camping trip. According to Suzy, she'd been helping Reese pack for his excursions for years. So she not only knew what was needed, she had it in stock.

There were energy bars and bottled water in that pack, Pam remembered, as her stomach gave a loud growl. But if she didn't find a place to relieve her bladder, her air mattress was going to become a raft. She reluctantly crawled towards the tent flap to go outside.

The sight that greeted her took her mind off her needs for a moment. A full moon cast a beautiful, clear light over the camping area, almost as bright as day. But just as Pam was caught up in the beauty, she realized it was going to be that much harder to find a place to do her private thing.

She knew within reason that Reese was asleep. There was no sign of him, so he must be in his tent sleeping like a baby, she thought resentfully. But what if he woke up and saw her? Which was silly, she reasoned. After all, he'd seen her totally nude in the hotel room in Vegas. But that was different.

Finally she made her way to the large rock she'd sat on earlier in the afternoon. It came almost to her waist, so she could at least hunker behind it. Boy, what she'd give for some of the toilet tissue in her pack. She hated to have to drip dry.

After finishing, she decided she'd try to find her pack. She could see that a Coleman stove had been set up and a pot was on it. Reese must have fixed himself something to eat. Again, resentment boiled up in her throat. He could at least have checked with her to see if she wanted anything.

Being as quiet as possible, she finally spotted her pack and was reaching down to lift it when a voice at her shoulder said, "Looking for anything in particular?"

The scream ripped unexpectedly from her throat, surprising her as much as it did Reese. And then she hit him. Her balled-up fist landed in the middle of his abdomen, almost knocking the air from his lungs. All the pent up fury she'd felt for the past twenty-four hours seemed to flow from her as one blow followed another until Reese managed to encircle her wrists with his big hands.

"Stop it, Pam!" he yelled. "Get hold of yourself! Pam! Oh, Pam, don't do that!"

But it was too late. As he gathered her to the same broad chest she'd just been pummeling, the flood of tears was already soaking the front of his shirt.

When her tears finally started to subside, Reese gently guided Pam to a foldout chair she hadn't noticed before.

"Sit here and I'll get you something to eat. You must be starved. You barely touched your food at lunch."

So he had paid a little attention to her, she thought, as she wiped her eyes with the paper towel he handed her from the table.

"I thought you were just sulking in the tent, so I didn't tell you when the food was done," Reese said, handing her a bowl of chili and some crackers. "Then when you didn't come out, I peeked in and realized you were asleep. I figured you needed the sleep more than the food."

"Thank you," she murmured, taking the food from him. What's up with him, now, she wondered, savoring the first few bites of the chili and crackers. This was good! Tasted like it was made from scratch! But why was he suddenly being nice to her? She slid a clandestine glance at him sitting in a foldout chair like the one she was in.

"You like the chili?" he asked, capturing her gaze, which she'd hoped he wouldn't notice.

"Yes! It tastes more like homemade than out of a can."

"More of Suzy's handiwork. She knows what my favorite foods are and tries to keep them on hand for my trips. She makes this chili and cans it, so I can bring some with me."

"She really loves you, Reese. I think you're like a son to her."

"Yeah, she's the only mom I've ever had." Pam was surprised at the tenderness in his voice.

"But I don't want to get all mushy and sentimental right now. If you're finished eating, I want to show you something."

He set the bowl back on the table and held out his hand to her. Almost suspicious of his friendly gesture, Pam hesitantly placed her hand in his and allowed him to pull her from the chair and lead her behind the tents toward the rock wall that loomed straight up. Moonlight glistened around them, turning their world into a mystical gray haze.

Pam thought Reese was going to walk directly into the rock wall when, unexpectedly, he made an abrupt turn and guided her through a narrow passageway that was barely wide enough for them to pass through single file. Still holding her hand, they walked for several feet before he made another turn and came to a stop.

Pam could only stare at the scene before her. A solid rock wall encircled a space that formed a completely hidden area that looked to be about 30 feet in diameter. Moonlight reflected off of and enhanced a small waterfall that cascaded down the rock wall to create a crystal clear pool that took up about half the area. She felt as if she'd stepped into her own fantasy paradise. This was the water she'd heard earlier, she realized, as she watched it tumble gently over the rocks to land in the pool before overflowing into a lower section to disappear again into the ground.

"Do you like it?" Reese's voice startled her. She'd been so caught up in the beauty surrounding her that she'd forgotten about him.

She made several attempts to get her words to come through the emotion that choked her vocal chords. "Oh, Reese! This is the most beautiful place I've ever seen. It's a hidden paradise!"

"I'm glad you think that. It's also a great natural shower. I thought you might like to refresh yourself after the long hot day you've had."

"You mean get in the water now? At night?"

"Sure, why not?"

"Well, how deep is the pool? And what about snakes and animals and things?"

"Typical woman!" Reese laughed. "We're perfectly safe here. I've been here before. The pool is about six feet at the deepest, right under the waterfall, but it gradually slopes down, so you don't have to worry about going in over your head too soon. And I can assure you that any snakes or "things" won't bother you here. But we can explore it more in the daylight. Right now, I thought we could just get under the waterfall and refresh ourselves a little. It'll be cold, but after you get used to it, you'll love it."

"Just walk into the water with our clothes on?" Pam looked up at him questioningly.

"Oh, no. We'll take our clothes off first. Haven't you ever been skinny dipping?" His teasing eyes glowed in the moonlight, causing Pam's breath to stop halfway in her chest.

"Excuse me?" She finally found her voice enough to whisper.

"Now don't get all prim and proper on me, Pam. This is our honeymoon, remember? Fifi said there *must* be a honeymoon. And since we've already consummated our marriage, there's no reason for you to be bashful about taking a shower with your husband."

Pam caught frantically at his wrists to try to stop him from unbuttoning her shirt. But his nimble fingers already had half the buttons undone.

"Reese! Stop this!" she hissed. "I'm not going to strip off and get in this water with you!"

"You don't have to do a thing, Darlin'. I'm going to do it all for you," he whispered, as his lips claimed hers in a hungry kiss.

By now her shirt was totally unbuttoned. Reese's hands were hot on her bare skin as he slipped them inside her open shirt and encircled her waist, drawing her closer to him as he deepened the kiss.

Chapter 11

Engulfed with desire at what Reese's hands and lips were doing to her, Pam allowed him to slowly undress her before removing his own clothes. On legs that felt as if they would give away under her at any moment, she let him guide her into the cold waterfall.

"You look like an Amazon princess with the water and moonlight playing over your hair and body," Reese growled, his lips once again claiming hers. "But wait, I want to look at you some more." He backed away from her just the slightest, to give himself a better view.

Pam knew she should feel the need to cover herself. But the flame in Reese's eyes told her he found her beautiful, releasing a newfound joy in her. Joy to be alive in this wonderful place. And joy to be making love to the only man she had ever loved.

So she gave herself to him, willingly, eagerly, when he gently cupped a breast in his hand and lowered his mouth to it. A wild

117

freedom overcame her as they made love in the moonlit water that spilled over them. She felt as if they were the only two people in the world. And if she thought she loved him before, there was no doubt now.

He might be one of the biggest jerks she'd ever known, but he was also one of the most gentle, tender people she'd ever known. And that was the part she would always love. The tender Reese. The achingly gentle Reese. Her husband. Her lover.

When they got back to camp, Reese led her into the big tent. "You didn't really think I was going to let you sleep in that little tent all by yourself, did you?"

"But why did you bring two air mattresses, if we aren't going to use but one?"

"Just in case I get tired of you. I might throw you out of my bed if you don't keep pleasing me," he teased.

"Oh, you—" but his lips hushed her retort as he pulled her down beside him and proceeded to love her again.

When Pam awoke the next morning Reese was gone. Disappointment engulfed her. Surely after what they'd shared last night, he could spend a little time with her. At least have breakfast with her.

She boiled some water on the Coleman stove and made a cup of instant coffee. She ate a breakfast bar while remembering the night before. They'd made love three times during the night. Reese was insatiable once he'd gotten started. But she sure wasn't complaining, she thought, a contented smile playing on her lips.

"Well, I hate to interrupt someone who looks so happy." The voice startled Pam into a standing position.

The man speaking to her wore what appeared to be a forest ranger's uniform. "But you can't stay here," he continued. His face was pleasant and he spoke with a smile, but authority carried in his every word.

"Excuse me?" was all Pam's surprised voice could get out.

"This is private property that you're camped on, and you have to move. I'll show you where the public camping areas are after you've broken camp here. It'll take you a little while to pack up your tents, so I'll come back in a couple of hours and show you where to go," he said, turning to leave.

"But wait! What do you mean, private property? I'm here with my husband and he's the one who chose this spot. Besides that, I can't leave without him, and I don't have any idea when he'll get back to camp."

"Oh? And what is he doing all day?" Sudden suspicion clouded the man's friendly features.

"He says he's filming eagles," Pam answered, hoping Reese didn't mind her telling a total stranger what he was doing. But this stranger had the power to make them leave, so she had to tell him.

"Hmmm. Filming eagles. I know someone who does that," he mused, with a crooked grin. "But that doesn't matter, you have to go." Again the firmness was back. "I don't think Reese would appreciate me allowing someone to camp on his land."

"Excuse me?" Pam repeated her first words to him. The man was going to think she was daft, but did she hear him correctly? "Who did you say this land belongs to?"

"I didn't say," he answered, casting her a shrewd glance.

"Yes, you did. You said someone wouldn't appreciate you letting me camp on their land."

"Oh! Did I say that out loud?" Again he grinned. Pam couldn't help but like the guy. If he had on different clothes, she was sure he'd look like an American Indian. Maybe he was. This was truly Indian country.

"Yes, I think the name you used was Reese."

"Yes, I probably did. And that's right, Reese wouldn't like a stranger being here."

"Would this by any chance be Reese Bainbridge you're referring to?" Pam asked, almost afraid of the answer.

"Sure would! You know him?" Now the grin was spread all over the man's tanned face.

"I guess you could say that," she answered, with a sinking feeling in the pit of her stomach. "I'm his wife."

Whaaaat? Don't tell me ol' Reese finally caved in and got married?"

"Seems like he did," she answered.

"But wait. How do I know you're not lying to me? Why would Reese camp out here, although I do know that he loves this place, when you could be staying in his house?" Unexpectedly he let out a whoop of a laugh and slapped his legs, as if he'd just heard the funniest thing in his life. "That's just like Reese. He's one of the richest men around, but he can't get the wild blood out of his veins. That boy has always loved the outdoors more than anyone I know."

Very slowly, Pam lowered herself into a chair. What was she hearing? That Reese owned this land? That he even had a house here? What was going on? What kind of game was he playing with her?

"Lady, you don't look so happy all of a sudden." The ranger had stopped laughing and had come closer to Pam. "In fact, you don't look real well at all. Are you okay? Have I upset you about something?"

"So you're telling me that Reese Bainbridge owns this land? He even owns a house close by? How long have you known him?"

"Oh crap! I've done it again, haven't I? I've talked too much. You didn't know about the land and house?" The look on his face, now, was one of fear.

"No. I didn't know," she admitted. "In fact, we're on our honeymoon and just got here yesterday."

"Well, I'm sure Reese has a reason for this. He's probably just testing you, to see if you like the outdoors as much as he does," he offered.

"What is your name?" Pam asked.

"John Littlefoot. Reese and I are cousins."

"Cousins?" Pam blurted. This just got better and better!

"Look, I gotta go. I've already said too much. I wish to hell I could persuade you not to even mention to Reese that I've been by here, but I know you'll tell him. And now I may be in deep crap with him. Man! I sure don't want to get his Indian blood stirred up." And before Pam could say another word, he'd disappeared into the underbrush.

Indian blood? Had he said *Indian* blood? How many more surprises would she have had if the man had stayed another thirty minutes?

Too numb to think, Pam headed for the waterfall. Maybe the cold water would clear her mind. But it didn't help. The stimulation just made her thoughts whirl faster.

How could Reese have been so loving to her last night, knowing all the time that he was deceiving her? What else was he keeping from her? Well, as soon as he came back to camp tonight he was in for a few big surprises. He had some questions to answer! How dare he deceive her like this!

Like you did him? The little voice interrupted her mental ranting. *At least he didn't deceive you into marrying him,* the inner voice continued. *He hasn't tried to move in and take over your heritage.*

"All right, already!" she yelled out loud. "I get the message!" And she did. She realized she didn't blame Reese for keeping his secrets. She could see his point. For all he knew she'd try to stake a claim on part of everything he owned, so she couldn't fault him for protecting himself from her. When she put herself in his shoes, she could very well understand why he'd be suspicious of her.

But she truly didn't want anything from the Bainbridges except to get Tom's life back. Somehow she had to make Reese understand that. But how? Now that they were married, he would never believe she hadn't meant to trick him into this situation from the beginning.

There's always divorce, the ever-present little voice whispered. Pam wanted to reach inside her head and rip that voice out and smash it, but she knew it was right, yet again. She knew instantly what she must do.

Fiona's will stated that there must be a honeymoon. But it didn't make any further stipulations. So she'd give Fiona a honeymoon. She'd give herself a honeymoon. But when it was over, she'd give Reese his freedom.

Fiona could rest in peace, knowing that her precious company was in good hands. Tom would have his life back. Reese would have his freedom. And she would have—she would have the most wonderful honeymoon she could ever have dreamed of. And, after that, maybe she would be able to stand the lonely life that would follow.

Having made up her mind that she wouldn't say anything to Reese about John Littlefoot's visit and her newfound knowledge, Pam set about to prepare supper.

When Reese returned to camp, he was amazed to find potatoes that Pam had rolled in tinfoil and baked by building a smoldering fire on the ground, letting it die down to coals, then placing the potatoes in the coals and letting them cook. She had made cornbread cakes and heated a can of pork and beans.

"Well, aren't we full of surprises," he murmured, pulling her close and kissing her neck.

Biting her tongue to keep from commenting about what had been on her mind all day, and that he was the one full of surprises, she said, "There's a lot you don't know about me, Reese."

"I know. But I plan to learn it all. Little by little, inch by inch," he whispered, starting to unbutton her shirt.

"But, Reese, the food!" she protested, half-heartedly.

"The food can wait, baby, I've been starving for you all day." His mouth claimed hers, to prove his point.

"Then why—?"

"Shhhh. No more talking. Concentrate on what you're feeling. That's all that matters right now." If he only knew how prophetic his words were.

Darkness was settling in when they finally sat down to eat. As the moon cast its silvery spell around them, Pam watched Reese's features as he talked about his day. *Indian blood?* She could see it now. The sharp, chiseled features. The dark hair. Throw in Fiona's flashing blue eyes, and Reese Bainbridge was a fascinating man to behold.

As the campfire died out and the moonlight played across his face, Pam sensed a wildness that lay just beneath the surface of the man facing her. A determination to never be tamed. A need to be his own person, no matter who wanted to own him. To claim him. She knew, without the shadow of a doubt, that if any woman ever claimed Reese Bainbridge it would be because he gave himself to her. Not because she demanded that he be hers. Fiona had witnessed his determination to never be forced to live a life he hated.

She also knew, in that instant, that she loved Reese too much to try to force him to be happy in a marriage he didn't want. This substantiated the decision she'd made earlier in the day, to let him go. If you love something—or someone—set them free. Oh, how she hoped he'd come back to her. But in her heart, she knew he wouldn't.

Feeling the beginning of an emptiness she didn't think she could bear, she went to him. Kneeling in front of him, she slid her arms around his waist and rested her head on his chest for the briefest of moments.

"What's this?" he asked in surprise.

"Shhhh," she repeated his words to him. "Concentrate on what you're feeling. That's all that matters right now." She slowly unbuttoned his shirt. Kissing her way down until his belt buckle stopped her. She could already feel him responding to her, and when she unfastened his belt and pants, she heard the sharp hiss of air as he sucked in his breath. She didn't stop until he was exhausted from her lovemaking.

Later, as they lay in the tent, Reese said, "You asked me once if I'd ever made love to a real woman. I can answer that question now.

Not until you. I've never known a woman as passionate and loving as you are."

"And you said it was obvious I'd never made love to a real man," Pam smiled. "And you were right. In fact, I'd never made love to a man at all. My only sexual contact before you was the jerk who raped me when I was just a teenager."

"You mean—?"

"Yes. Technically, you're the first man I've ever made love to," she answered quietly.

"Well, I have to admit we're experiencing some real fine sex. But I'm not sure that love has anything to do with it," Reese answered, honestly.

"It has *everything* to do with it for me," Pam said, turning her head away from him, trying to hide the tear that slid silently down her face. "Otherwise, I wouldn't be doing it."

"I believe you, Pam," he whispered, turning her face back to him and kissing the tear from her cheek. "But I'm still a little confused about our entire situation, so I was making the statement for myself."

He pulled her close in his arms and, for the moment, she felt warm and loved and protected. Let tomorrow bring what it would, she thought, as she drifted into a contented sleep.

Chapter 12

"I saw John Littlefoot today," Reese said, holding Pam's gaze.

"Who?" She hoped her voice sounded sincere. She finished storing the food so it wouldn't attract varmints to the camp. Supper was finished, and it was her favorite time of the day. Sitting around the campfire with Reese, listening to him talk, loving his relaxed state, and anticipating the moment he would take her hand and lead her into the tent for their magical lovemaking.

"Don't try to play it off, Pam. He told me everything the two of you discussed. He was very apologetic for spilling his guts to you."

A week had passed since John Littlefoot had come by the camp. Reese and Pam had settled into a routine. He was gone when she awoke every morning. She had supper ready when he came home at night. Sometimes they made love before they ate, and sometimes they made love after they ate. But not a night had passed that they hadn't made love at least once. Several times, Reese had loved her awake during the middle of the night. Those times were the most precious to Pam. She gloried in the thought of him waking up and needing to touch her. To be near her.

"When were you going to tell me?" Reese's voice interrupted her thoughts.

"Probably never," she shrugged.

"Why?"

"Why would I? It's obvious you didn't want me to know this is your land, or that you own a house here, or you would have told me."

"It's not like it seems. I planned to tell you."

"It's okay, Reese. I can understand your reasons for not telling me."

"Oh? And what are those reasons?"

"You think I tricked you into marrying me to get your house and money, so it's perfectly understandable that you'd want to keep this a secret so I wouldn't try to get my hands on it, too."

"Don't ever try to read my mind, Pam. It won't work." For the first time in many days, Pam detected the old hardness in Reese's voice. He got up and threw more wood on the campfire, causing sparks to fly into the air before dancing into oblivion.

"But I really do understand—"

"No. You don't understand, because you don't have any idea what I've been doing." He returned to his chair.

"You've been taking pictures of eagles, haven't you? That's what you said you were going to do."

"Yes, that's what I said, and I've been doing that, too, for a magazine article I'm writing. But that's not my main reason for being here this trip. I'm finishing a book that I have to have done in another week. I have a deadline for the end of this month, with a hotshot publisher who wants this one and maybe another one."

"A book on eagles?"

"No, I'm afraid not," he answered with a chuckle.

"Then what is it about?" Pam persisted.

"My ancestors."

"You're doing a family tree?" Now Pam was really puzzled.

"Kind of. It's about my Indian ancestors."

"Oh!"

"John didn't bother to mention to you that I'm part American Indian, did he?" Was that a look of apprehension in those flashing blue eyes?

"Well, he said he sure didn't want to get your Indian blood stirred up. So I didn't know if he was sincere, or just joking."

"He was very sincere. He looks more the part than I do, because his mom married an Indian. So he's three quarters Cherokee, and I'm only one quarter."

"Was Fiona part Indian?"

"No. This was on my mom's side. My mom was half Cherokee. She was a descendent of the Eastern Band of Cherokee Indians. Do you know anything about the Trail of Tears?" As he talked, a quiet reverence crept into Reese's voice. As if he were speaking of things sacred. As if he thought the spirits of his ancestors might be sitting in the shadows listening to his story to see if he would tell it correctly.

"I remember studying a little about the Trail of Tears in school." Unexpectedly, she felt guilty that she could remember so little about a subject that seemed so important to Reese.

"That's the reason my publisher wants this book. He thinks I'm on to an idea that can be used as assigned reading in History classes that will make the story come alive and live longer in people's minds. My book is fiction, but it's based on complete facts of things that happened to the Indians who were driven from their land and forced to live on reservations."

"So was your mom on a reservation?"

"No. As I said, her ancestors became known as the Eastern Band. Her great-great-grandparents hid in these mountains when, in 1838, the federal government came and forced most Cherokees to go west to Oklahoma. They managed to keep this very land that we sit on right now, and it's been passed down through my ancestors until now. I'm the last surviving member from my mom's family, so if I don't have children, I plan to leave my land to John Littlefoot's children. Our grandfathers were brothers, so we're second cousins."

Darkness had settled in around them. The only light was the campfire that flickered eerie shadows against the trees and under-brush surrounding them. Some of the shadows almost looked like ghostly bodies hunkering around to listen to Reese's story.

A shiver ran over Pam. She tried to hide it from Reese, but his ever-watchful eyes caught the action, and he moved closer to her and took her hand in his.

"Does it bother you that I'm part Indian?"

"Oh, Reese! Not at all. I'm intrigued with your story. I want to hear more about the Trail of Tears. It sounds so terrible."

"It was atrocious. It's one of the saddest episodes of our Ameri-can history. What it boils down to is that white settlers moving into the areas pressed the U.S. government to do something about the Indians, because the whites just didn't want them around. So in 1825, the government formally adopted a removal policy, which was carried out in the 1830s by President Andrew Jackson and President Martin

Van Buren. So, as a result, the Indians of the southeastern United States—primarily the Cherokee, Chickasaw, Choctaw, Creeks, and Seminoles—were moved hundreds of miles to a new home."

"But that's horrible!" Pam protested.

"Horrible doesn't come close to describing the conditions these people were made to endure. They were taken from their land and forced to march a thousand miles. Some made part of the trip by boat in equally horrible conditions. Thousands died on the trip. That's why it's called The Trail Of Tears."

"But if they were forced to leave, how did your people wind up with this land?"

"As I said earlier, my mother's people became part of what's known as the Eastern Band. Prior to the Trail of Tears, a small group of Cherokees in western North Carolina had received permission to be excluded from the move west. This group was often called the Oconaluftee Indians. They didn't live on Cherokee Nation land and considered themselves separate from the Cherokee Nation. Also, a few of the Cherokees just refused to be removed, so they hid in the mountains around here and managed to escape the soldiers and spies who hunted for them. My mother's people were in the few that managed to escape the removal. Many of those in hiding were eventually allowed to settle among the Cherokees of western North Carolina. That was the beginning of the Eastern Band of Cherokees."

"Did Fiona know about all of this?"

"Ah, yes. Fiona knew. And she hated every aspect of it. She hated that her son had married a "half-breed," as I once heard her yelling at him. She hated it that my mom owned land here, because she was afraid that would lure my parents back here. And she hated it that my mom's blood runs strong in my veins, calling me here, making me want to spend hours, days, weeks, exploring these hills. I love taking photos of everything that exists in these mountains. I love just sitting, breathing in the very spirit of the history that hovers over this land. Yes, Fiona knew this. And she hated it to the point that she would do *anything* to get me back to Dallas, to her manmade, concrete world.

"When my mom died in the car accident, she was on her way back from here to get me. She'd made arrangements with John's parents to live with them until she could find a place for us to live."

The fire had died down to smoldering embers, allowing the darkness of the night to crowd closer and closer. Lightning flashed in the distance and a soft roll of thunder followed it.

"But enough history for tonight." Reese's voice broke the silence. "It's gotten hotter since the sun went down, I believe. I think from the look and feel of things we're in for a storm. Why don't we go to the falls and cool off a little." He reached for Pam's hand and pulled her from her chair.

Instant heat washed through her body, and it had nothing to do with the pending storm. Anticipation caused her pulses to accelerate with a throbbing that coursed through her being. She could already feel Reese's hands on her, touching, caressing, bringing her pleasures that she'd never known existed.

Clouds had covered the moon, so the only light was from a flashlight Reese had grabbed as they left the camp. It cast an eerie circle of light on the path in front of them, but everywhere else was pitch black, giving Pam the impression she was being led into some dark cave by her Indian captor. The thought caused a nervous giggle to rise in her throat.

"Care to share the joke?" Reese's voice shattered the dark night.

"It's nothing," she covered. "I think I'm just nervous tonight, since it's so dark. Are you sure this is safe?"

By now they were to the edge of the waterfall. Reese shined the light around to make sure nothing hovered close to harm them, then snapped the light off and reached for Pam.

"Tonight I'm going to teach you to be one with the universe. When it's totally black like this, there's no visual to distract from our concentration. Just feelings. Sensations. Being. Just be, tonight, Pam. Feel my hands on you as I touch you. Let the sensations sear your mind. Feel how hot with passion my hands are on your flesh. Touch me back, Pam. Let me feel, too." His voice was low, as if he didn't want to disturb the night.

His whispered, passionate words and his hands on her body drove Pam to a point that she had never been. It felt so right, so primal, to have him take her here on the cool grass, with the sound of the water falling around them.

There was a difference in his lovemaking tonight. Almost as if sharing his history with her had freed him of a bondage that had held him back until now. There was a wildness, an abandonment that she had never experienced in him. And her own spirit met his—matched his, as they celebrated the night with their love.

Almost too exhausted to move, Reese took Pam's hand and helped her to her feet. Again he flashed the light around to make certain his footsteps were sure as he led her into the falling water. The cool water chilled her hot flesh, causing a shiver to run over her body. But Reese's lips on hers turned the shiver into a tremor of a totally different nature.

"I just don't seem to be able to get enough of you," his lips whispered against hers. When she opened her mouth to respond, he claimed it before she could get a word out.

And he proved, yet again, that he couldn't get enough of her. As they reached their pinnacle at the same time a flash of lightning rent the sky, illuminating their bodies in the falling water, and for a brief moment Pam thought they looked like a statue of two lovers caught unaware.

The fierce clap of thunder that followed the lightning let them know the storm was on them.

"We'd better get back to the tent and make sure everything is tied down and safe," Reese said, leading her out of the water.

By now the lightning was so continuous that they didn't need the flashlight to light the way. By the time they reached camp the wind was blowing so hard they had to lean into it just to walk.

"This is not good!" Reese yelled, dodging something that flew by his head. He drew Pam closer to him, to protect her. Finally they made it to the tent and dove in for shelter.

The trees overhead moaned and swayed under the assault of the wind. The lightning was constant and the thunder so loud that Pam, who usually loved storms, clamped her hands over her ears to shield them from the noisy onslaught. She could tell Reese was truly concerned as he gathered her close to him and positioned his body over hers to protect her in case one of the huge trees decided to give way under the wind.

"I think it's blowing over," he yelled between claps of thunder.

Pam smiled and nodded her head, hoping he was correct. She studied his face in the flashing lightning. A face that would be burned into her mind's eye for as long as she lived. A face that she had grown to love to the point of distraction. A face that would soon be just a memory. So she studied it. Memorized it. Etched it into her subconscious so that on dark, lonely nights she could conjure it up and remember the brief, wonderful time she'd had loving this man.

She fell asleep fearing, dreading the future.

Chapter 13

Pam awoke to the sound of soft rain falling on the tent. But the wind had stopped blowing so hard. And it was light outside. Slowly she became aware that she wasn't alone. Turning her head slightly, she looked into Reese's blazing blue eyes.

"You know, you're a constant surprise to me," he said, running his thumb over her sleep-swollen lips.

"I am?" She was so surprised to find him still here with her this morning that she couldn't think of much more to say.

"Yes. You are. Every other woman I know would have been in hysterics last night during that storm. But you had the audacity to fall asleep in the middle of it!" Wonder and just a little awe tinged his voice, to Pam's surprise.

"Well, I just happen to love storms. Although that one last night was a little too much to really *love*."

She expected anything except his booming laugh. "You love storms? I didn't know that about you, Pam."

"There are a lot of things you don't know about me, Reese," Pam whispered, wanting to tell him that one of those things was that she loved him so much she'd do anything to make him happy.

"Hmmm. Want to elaborate on a few?" he teased, sliding his hand down her throat to let it stop and rest gently cupping a breast.

"Well, for one thing—"

"Um-hmm," he whispered.

Pam was aware of the rain quietly pelting the tent, and Reese's mouth lowering to replace his hand. Sweet, delicious sensations shot through her body as his mouth covered her peak.

"Reese, I can't talk with you doing that," she groaned.

"I know. So don't talk just yet. We'll continue this conversation later."

Later—much later—Reese handed Pam a cup of coffee. It had stopped raining long enough for them to make coffee and find a few things to eat that hadn't blown away in the storm. But the rain had started back, so they sat cross-legged on the bed to drink the coffee and eat some stale raisin bread that had managed to make it through the storm.

"So, tell me all those things about you that I don't know," he picked up where they'd been a long while ago. "For starters, tell me how a city girl like you came to be so comfortable in a tent during a raging storm. Why weren't you screaming hysterically?"

"Well, I've spent about as much time in tents as I have being a city girl," she started to explain. "When Tom and I were kids, and even after we were teenagers, our dad thought the ideal summer vacation was to spend it traveling through different parts of the country. Camping and 'living off the land,' as he used to say. And I don't mean a week or two. I mean the entire summer! So I've done my time in tents, under about all the weather conditions there are."

When they'd first arrived here, Pam thought she'd love it when the time came for her to let Reese know that his punishment for her was something she was quite comfortable with. She thought, then, that she'd feel jubilation at putting him in his place when the time came. But now she only wanted to share the knowledge with him. She had no desire to get back at him.

But to her astonishment she could feel him withdrawing from her.

"Reese? What's wrong?" She was almost afraid to ask.

"Wrong?" For the first time in weeks she heard the old familiar hardness in his voice. Got a glimpse of the Reese that she'd almost forgotten about.

"Wrong? Oh, nothing's wrong. And I shouldn't even be surprised to find out just one more little underhanded trait of Pam Spencer. Oh—I almost forgot. It's Pam Bainbridge now, isn't it?"

"Reese! What are you talking about? Why are you angry with me?"

"Why didn't you tell me you knew how to live this kind of life?" His voice was controlled fury.

"You didn't ask, Reese. You brought me here thinking you were going to really punish me for all of my sins by letting me rot in this camp, day in and day out, alone, so now you're angry because your little scheme didn't work? Is that it?"

"And I guess you were laughing at me behind my back all the time, weren't you?"

"You know what? Actually, after a couple of days, I forgot about it. I just settled in and enjoyed being here, but I'm sure you won't believe that."

"You actually enjoyed it?" He was almost shouting now, but for some reason the situation was suddenly funny to Pam. It was almost like the story of Brer Rabbit being thrown into the briar patch.

But as Reese rose and stormed from the tent all humor evaporated from Pam. For some reason he was very angry about the situation. Pam slowly followed him from the tent. The rain still drizzled a little, but it went unnoticed as she made her way to him.

"Reese? Why are you so angry about this?"

"Look," he said, not even glancing at her, "everything is ruined. If you knew so much about camping, why didn't you store the food so that it couldn't get wet, like this?" He dumped soggy crackers, bread, and other items onto the ground at her feet.

"Damn you, Reese Bainbridge!" Pam's voice was quiet, controlled fury. She'd had enough. Enough of his on again, off again attitude toward her. Enough of loving him so much her entire body ached, but hurting even more when he turned on her like this.

Stunned at her words, Reese slowly turned to face her. He was even more stunned at the cold rage he saw blazing in her green eyes.

"Don't you *dare* try to put the blame for this on me. After all, you're the one who's been sitting in a house all day. You probably heard a weather forecast and knew we were in for storms. So just shut up about it!"

Gradually Pam became aware of the sound of sheets of rain in the trees, approaching them. She made a dash for the tent and barely made it in before Reese crashed in behind her. One of his feet tangled with hers and they both plummeted onto the air mattress. A sudden POP-WHOOSH rent the air as the valve in the mattress popped open from their weight hitting it so hard.

The hissing sound of escaping air was more than Pam could take. Hysterical laughter pealed from her throat, sapping her of the anger she'd been overcome with a few minutes earlier. She lay on her back with Reese's body half covering hers, his face buried in the crook of her neck. She felt him start to chuckle, and she laughed even harder.

Reese rolled onto his back and together they roared with laughter. Each time they thought they were over it, one would giggle or chuckle, and they'd start all over again. Each time one of them moved and more air hissed from the mattress, their laughter got harder. Finally they lay exhausted and relaxed on the flat, airless mattress.

The rain still fell in torrents, but as Reese propped up on one elbow and looked down at Pam she was only aware of his closeness, and how wonderful he looked with the remnants of laughter still lingering in his eyes.

Very slowly, his eyes locked with hers, he lowered his lips until they covered hers in a tender kiss. Pam was instant in her desire for him. She couldn't imagine another man ever turning her on like Reese Bainbridge did. Her hand slid up around his neck to pull him closer, but he captured it in the hand that lay behind her head, holding her in a position in which she was helpless to do anything but lay imprisoned under his blue blaze.

Slowly, deliberately, he started unbuttoning the shirt she had hastily thrown on, without a bra, when she'd followed him from the tent. Tantalizingly he undid each button, leaving the material where it lay, until he reached the last button, savoring what lay beneath until he could uncover it at his leisure.

Pam's breath came in short puffs as she watched, anticipated, longed for him to claim the treasure he was so carefully unwrapping.

Her entire body throbbed with the desires he was evoking. She wanted to scream for him to hurry, yet wanted him to continue his torture of her. Oh! The sweet torture!

She sucked in air as he raised his hand and carefully pulled her shirt away from one breast, exposing it just enough for him to look at it before lowering his mouth to claim it. She thought she would die with the pleasure he was bringing to her. Just when she thought she could take no more, she felt his hand slide slowly down her body. Closer and closer it came to the top of her pants. Teasing, circling, working its way inside her jeans, downward to the center of her universe.

"Reese—"

"Shhhh. I want to watch you. I want to see the pleasure on your face. Do this for me, Pam."

Gazing into his eyes, Pam responded to him with all the love she would ever know for another human being. As spasm after glorious spasm racked her body, she kept her eyes open, allowing Reese to see into her very soul. She might not be able to say the words to him, but if he could see inside her soul, surely he could see the love she felt for him.

Later, as they lay exhausted from making love, they realized the rain had stopped and the sun was shining.

"Well, as much as I hate to end this, I think we'd better make a trip to the waterfalls and freshen up, then start packing this stuff up," Reese said, rising from the flat mattress.

"Pack up?"

"Yes. We're staying at the house for the rest of this trip."

Chapter 14

Pam stopped abruptly. What lay in front of her took her breath away. After what seemed like a very short walk farther up the mountainside, they stood about three hundred yards from one of the most spectacular log homes she had ever seen. It looked more like a hunting lodge than an individual dwelling. Snuggled in a clump of huge oak trees, it was almost camouflaged as trees and sky reflected off of myriad windows that seemed more evident than the logs.

"It's beautiful, Reese! But being the nature lover that you seem to be, I'm surprised you destroyed trees to build your house."

"Good point, Pam," Reese chuckled. "But I used what are called 'standing dead logs.'" Noticing Pam's uncomprehending look, he continued, "Standing dead logs are trees that are no longer living or growing but have remained standing for long periods of time, for whatever reason. There are many forests of standing dead trees.

141

Sometimes fire will kill the trees, but not damage them enough to keep them from being used for logs to build with. There are a lot of other things that can kill them, too. A lot of these logs came from out west."

Before Pam could comment, Reese's Jeep came roaring around the house and screeched to a stop not far from them. Sharon Anderson, wearing short-shorts and a halter-top, jumped from the truck and headed toward the house. She hadn't noticed Reese and Pam.

Pam couldn't believe her eyes as Sharon used a key to open the front door and let herself into Reese's home.

"Now, Pam," Reese started, seeing the look of horror on Pam's face. "This isn't what it looks like. She's here working. She's typing my manuscript as I write it. I hate sitting in front of a computer and writing, so I do my writing on notepads and Sharon puts it into the computer."

"How long has she been here?" Pam felt anger and dismay warring inside her. Had this bimbo been at his house with him every day, while she sat at that miserable campsite with nothing to occupy her time?

"She got here the day after we did," he answered reluctantly. "But, Pam, before you make a big deal out of this, you have to remember that I had already made plans to come here and work before I found out about our marriage, much less our mandatory honeymoon. If I don't get this manuscript finished on time, I stand a chance of losing the contract with the publisher."

Pushing her hurt to the back of her mind in the face of his reasoning, Pam nodded her understanding.

"Now come on, we might as well get this over with," he said, taking her hand and pulling her toward the house.

Get this over with was right, Pam thought miserably as she allowed Reese to hold her hand and lead her up the tall steps to the huge, solid wood door. She didn't look forward to an encounter with Sharon.

But as Pam stepped through the door, she forgot about Sharon. She was overwhelmed with the emotions that engulfed her. Peace. A quiet and restful serenity, like nothing she had ever known, washed through her as she gazed at the warm, honey-colored logs that formed the walls. The windows opened up from every direction to expose the outside view to the point that it was hard to tell if one were inside or outside.

Everything on the first floor was open. The kitchen, dining area, living space, all blended into one huge, warm area with an enormous fireplace at one end. A plush, rust-brown leather couch, matching loveseat and recliner formed a nook around the fireplace. A round, solid oak dining room table, chairs and cabinet were placed beside windows overlooking a valley where deer grazed, unafraid.

A spiral staircase led up to the second floor bedrooms. Pam knew without seeing them that they would be as warm and inviting as the area where she now stood.

This house was as opposite of the house at Bainbridge Hall as Reese was opposite of Fiona. No wonder he loved being here so much. And I'm going to love being here, Pam thought.

Whoa! Where had that come from? Because she knew that even as much as this felt like home to her, she would never be allowed to stay here. Would never have the chance to snuggle up on one of those large couches in front of a big, warm fire on a cold winter's night with Reese and make plans for their future. Sadness formed a knot in the pit of her stomach as she glanced around the lovely house again, realizing that, yes, this was home—just not hers.

"Reese, is that you?" Sharon's voice preceded her down the staircase. "I thought I heard the door close. Are you home? Oh! There you are. I missed you this morning. You didn't come home at your usual time. I had your breakfast fixed and everything. I waited as long as I could before going into Cherokee to pick up some items. I—OH!" She'd finally spotted Pam, who'd been partially hidden behind a large potted palm tree.

"What is *she* doing here, Reese?" Sharon yelped. "You promised me you were going to keep her secluded in the camp while we were here. You said you didn't want her to ever see this house because she'd just want *it*, too! You said—"

"Sharon!" Reese bellowed. "Shut the hell up!" Pam had never seen him this angry. And she had never felt this hurt.

Sharon turned and stormed back up the stairs and slammed the door to some room.

"Come on, Pam, I want to show you where I work, and tell you a little about the book I'm writing."

Pam followed Reese up the beautiful, curving staircase onto a landing that also had a sitting area that looked down over the living room. One could sit up here and watch the fire in the fireplace below.

Reese led her to a room, and she suddenly felt as if she were standing in space. The room was round, with windows from floor to ceiling. A table and office chair sat close to a window. Papers, pens, books, and other items were spread around on the table.

"Come over here and see where I work," Reese said, again taking her hand and drawing her near the table.

Pam was overcome with the view. This room was apparently in the back of the house. It looked out over a spectacular valley. Pam could see no ground below the window, as if the room actually hung out over the valley.

"This is where I write most of the time. This is my inspiration. I sit here and look out at this view, and I can understand the sorrow of the people who were led from this area. And I can understand how some of them risked their lives to hide here, rather than be herded to a land they knew nothing of. I can understand how some of them would rather die here than live a life they hated."

"Like the life Fiona wanted you to live?"

"Yes."

"Are you saying that you would rather be dead here than alive and working at Bainbridge Corporation?"

"Look at my dad. He died an early death *because* he gave in to her. So what's the difference? So, yes, I'd rather be dead here than dead there!"

Pam was amazed at the conviction in his voice. She wondered if Fiona could ever have imagined how sincere he was about not being part of the family company.

She noticed an easel close to his worktable. It had a display of articles pinned to it that covered subjects in his book. Articles about how the Cherokee had a written language created by Sequoyah, who wanted his people to be educated. An article that said that by the early 1840s a Cherokee newspaper, *The Phoenix*, was being circulated throughout the territory. Clippings about how when Hernando de Soto came through the interior southeast of this country in 1540, he described large villages and towns based on farming. And how the Indians lived in log houses with fireplaces, and were very civilized.

Pam learned more about the Cherokee Indians by glancing through the articles than she'd ever known in her life. This book that Reese was writing was going to be very important. Suddenly she felt ashamed of the part she'd played in distracting him from the important work he was doing. Ashamed to have been part of Fiona's plan to trick him into becoming something he didn't want any part of.

"Well, this is probably boring you, so I'll show you the rest of the house." Reese's voice and hand on her arm interrupted her thoughts.

"No, I'm not bored at all, Reese. I find this fascinating," Pam said, feeling her heartbeat speed up at his close proximity.

"Really? Well, there might be hope for you after all," he teased, his breath warm on her cheek as he spoke.

She ached for him to kiss her. She couldn't be this close to him and keep her mind on anything except how his lips felt on hers. How his hands felt caressing her body. How she wanted to be a part of his life.

"Did you say it, Reese?" she asked, surprising both of them.

"Did I say what?" he asked, drawing back from her only slightly.

"That you didn't want me to see this house."

"Yes. I was very angry with you and Fiona for tricking me into this marriage and I did say it. But that was then. A lot of things have changed since then."

Before she could answer he captured her lips under his in a kiss that had the promise of things to come. His arms came around her and molded her body to his. She felt herself melting against him as her arms crept up around his neck. By the time the kiss ended, they were both panting for air. And wanting more to happen than just a kiss.

"And this is another reason that I didn't want you here," Reese's gruff voice whispered. "I won't be able to concentrate on a thing, just knowing that you're in this house."

"Well, then I'll leave," she whispered back, snuggling closer to him.

"Don't even think about it," he commanded. "I can't wait for night to get here, so I can get you into my bed."

"Why do we have to wait for night?" Pam teased, slowly running her hand down his body.

"Woman! I've got work to do! Now get out of here. Go look around. Amuse yourself. I'll see you later." He gave her a quick kiss on the lips and pushed her through the door.

Reluctantly, Pam made her way toward the stairs. Just as she reached the top step, about to make her way down, she stopped in mid-stride. From her view up here she could see out through the huge lower-level windows at what looked like miles and miles of trees, mountain ranges, and dipping valleys. This house apparently sat on a very tall mountain. She had never seen such a beautiful view in her entire life.

Slowly she made her way down the stairs, enjoying the changing view with each step she took. The architect who designed the house must have had this in mind.

"You might as well enjoy it while you can, because you won't be here long," Sharon's vindictive voice greeted Pam as she stepped from the last stair. Sharon's voice was deliberately low so Reese couldn't hear what she was saying.

"Oh? And why is that?" Pam asked.

"Because we don't want you here. You may have tricked Reese into marrying you, but he doesn't plan on staying married to you. Do you really think he's going to spend his life with a fat loser?" Bitterness cracked through her voice.

"Sharon, I don't think that what Reese and I do is any of your business. You're just a hired hand," Pam responded. She'd about had as much of this person as she could take.

"You fat bitch! You're going to regret the day you met the Bainbridges and got in my way! I'm the one he loves! I'm the one he's always loved. We'd be married if you and your money-grubbing brother hadn't come along." She stormed away before Pam could answer.

Oddly enough, Pam's anger dissipated almost instantly, to be replaced by a tiny apprehension. She'd never seen anyone as eaten up with anger and bitterness as Sharon was. And that last thing she'd thrown at Pam sure sounded like a threat. Oh, well, she'd worry about it if it happened, she decided. Right now, she wasn't going to think about it.

She found herbal tea bags in the kitchen and put a cup of water in the microwave. While waiting for the water to heat, Pam looked around at the spacious kitchen. Suddenly she had visions of her and Reese preparing a meal together while their children played around them. Maybe on a Saturday night, getting ready to have guests over for a cookout. Warmth washed over her at the cozy thought, but the shrill sound of the microwave brought her back to reality.

Taking her cup of tea, she sat at the dining room table and looked out over the valley below. Again a feeling of being home washed through Pam. She had lived in many places and had prided herself that she could be happy anywhere, but she had never been in a place that *felt* like home, like this place did. It wasn't just the house. It was the surroundings, too. It was as if she'd spent her entire life looking for this place. That she could grow old and die here.

Dream on, girl, the little voice inside said, bringing her abruptly out of her reverie. Just for a moment she'd forgotten she could never live in this house with Reese like a real husband and wife. She'd forgotten that she had to set him free. That she had, along with Fiona, cheated him out of the freedom he cherished so much. That she had trapped him into a life he didn't want, just like his ancestors had been entrapped and forced to live a life they didn't want.

All of a sudden it became of utmost importance to Pam that she leave this place. She must get away before she became more attached to it than she already was. She'd never felt the love for Bainbridge Hall that she did for this place. She never dreamed of, or wanted to live at Bainbridge Hall, so it would never have been a problem to walk away.

But after being with Reese for the past few weeks, after growing to love him in every way possible, and now already feeling an attachment to this house and land, she knew she had to go, or she would never be able to go on her own.

But how? How would she be able to get away without interfering with Reese's writing? She didn't want to slow him down any and cause him to miss his deadline.

Maybe Sharon could take her down to Cherokee and she could find a way to the airport. As much as she hated the thought of asking Sharon to do anything for her, that seemed to be the only way. She was sure Sharon would be happy to get rid of her.

She'd ask her right now. Maybe Sharon could even take her this afternoon. Urgency drove Pam to take her cup to the sink and rinse it out before heading up the stairs to find Sharon. Urgency made her determined to get out of this house before night. She couldn't spend the night with Reese and wake up in the morning here. If she did, she knew she'd never want to leave.

Hurrying up the stairs, Pam went in search of the room where Sharon worked at a computer. She was about to walk past Reese's room when words stopped her in her tracks.

"I'm telling you, Reese, she thinks she's going to live here. She says she loves this place." Sharon's voice almost convinced Pam that she really was concerned for Reese's welfare.

"Sharon, this isn't something you need to worry about. I'm a big boy. I can take care of myself and my house."

"But Reese—" now desperation tinged her whining voice—"I'm just concerned for you. You said that no woman would ever live in this house with you, but you just don't know how determined she is. She tricked you into marrying her so she could get your company and Bainbridge Hall. Now that she knows about this place, she wants it, too."

"Damn it, Sharon! You stress too much over things that don't concern you. I've made arrangements that will protect this house from anyone! From you, *and* from Pam. Nobody gets this house and land unless I change those arrangements. Pam may be able to get Bainbridge Hall, but she'll never be able to touch this house. So you need to just go back to work and finish typing what I've written!"

As they turned toward the door, they spotted Pam leaning against the doorframe listening to their conversation. Both stopped, their mouths open. Then a wicked, delighted smile spread over Sharon's face.

"Pam—" Reese came toward her with his hands outstretched.

Pam held her hands up to stop him. "Reese, you refuse to believe that I don't want your homes, your money, or anything that you have. You refuse to believe that all I've ever wanted was to get Tom's health back. You won't accept the fact that I was just as much a pawn in Fiona's hands as you were. She used me, Reese, to get to you. She—"

"HELLO? Anyone up there?" The voice came from the bottom of the stairs, interrupting Pam's outburst.

"John Littlefoot, is that you?" Reese called, brushing past Pam and heading for the stairs.

"That'll teach you to cross me," Sharon's waspish whisper grated as she, too, left the room.

Pam stood for a moment listening to the two men's booming voices coming from downstairs. What was she going to do? How was she going to get away from here? Because now she knew she *had* to get away.

"Sure, I'll take them to Cherokee for you, Cuz. You know I don't mind doing that." John's voice rang up the stairs loud and clear, giving Pam the answer she'd been desperately searching for.

Running to the room where Reese had put her personal belongings, Pam grabbed her wallet and a few other things that she'd need to travel with, but no bag or clothes. She stuck the items under her shirt, hoping she could hold onto them and get past Reese without him noticing. Neither man looked up as she quietly went down the stairs and out the front door.

She went to the side of John Littlefoot's 4-door Crew Cab pickup truck, which was faced away from the house. She desperately hoped she wouldn't be seen by anyone looking out the door or window. Testing the back door, she was relieved when it opened to her touch.

She crawled into the back seat and hunkered down and waited. Thankfully, the windows were slightly tinted, so it would be hard for anyone to spot her unless they were really looking. Now if Reese just wouldn't follow John out to the truck, all would be fine.

After what seemed a long, uncomfortable time, she heard voices as the two men came out the front door.

Stay away, she willed Reese. And to her great relief she heard him saying goodbye and that he would see John later.

John got into the truck without even looking in the back seat, started the truck and pulled out onto the road.

Pam wanted to get one last look at the house, but didn't dare raise up enough to look back at her quickly departing happiness. A lump the size of her fist settled into her midsection as she felt the truck smooth out onto the highway. Before she remembered to stop it, a groan slipped from her throat.

"What the hell?" John slammed on the brakes and guided the truck to a screeching halt beside the highway.

Chapter 15

Pam watched Dallas fading into the distance through her rearview mirror. She couldn't believe all that had happened in the two weeks since she'd left Reese's mountain.

It had taken all of her persuasive abilities to convince John Littlefoot to take her into Cherokee with him. His first determination was to take her back to Reese, but Pam finally made him realize that it was best for Reese's work if she left. So John had wound up taking her on to the airport in Ashville.

Her first stop had been to visit Tom and let him know she was okay and what she planned to do. He went with her to see Dan Smythe to make sure there were no clauses in the will that would keep her from divorcing Reese. Dan assured them that Tom's inheritance of Bainbridge Corporation was in place and would stay that way even if Reese and Pam divorced.

"She really thought if you two spent a honeymoon together, you'd realize you loved each other," he said to Pam. "She only wanted the best for Reese, you know. And she thought you were the best."

But, in the end, he agreed to start the divorce proceedings. Pam assured him she wanted nothing from Reese Bainbridge or the Bainbridge estate. She just wanted out. She just wanted to give Reese the thing that she had taken away from him—his freedom.

Then she had written Reese a long letter, telling him she had filed for divorce and that now maybe he and Sharon could be together like Sharon said they wanted to be.

Pam smiled slightly, remembering throwing that little zinger into the letter. She was pretty much convinced Reese didn't care for Sharon, but he needed to know Sharon had made that claim. It was also Pam's way of getting the last word in on Sharon, through Reese. But, she thought with a mental shrug, maybe Reese did want to marry Sharon. Good luck to both of them, she thought miserably.

So here she was heading into the west Texas sun, going nowhere. She'd let Tom talk her into taking his newly acquired Cadillac Escalade SUV and going on a driving trip for at least a year, or until she felt like she could come home and start life over.

"It's the least I can do, Pam," Tom insisted. "After all, you've pretty much screwed up your entire life for me, so at least take the Escalade and I'll give you a monthly allowance until you decide what you want to do."

She'd argued a little, but finally gave in. After all, she didn't want to be in Dallas if Reese decided to come and look for her. She didn't want to see him again until the divorce was final. In fact, it'd be better for her if she never saw him again. Just let the pain she felt from loving him and losing him wear itself down to a dull ache so she'd be able to live with it.

She'd made arrangements with Sam Winger to take a year's leave of absence from her job. Sam hadn't wanted her to be gone that long, but finally told her to get her life together and hurry back.

She was trying to make herself believe she'd enjoy an entire year of just driving and seeing the country. She planned to visit the few states her parents hadn't managed to take her and Tom to when they were kids.

Lightning ripped through a distant thunderhead, reminding Pam of the storm that she and Reese had endured in the tent, and of their tender lovemaking after the storm was over. A heartrending moan tore its way from her throat. Overcome with emotion, she pulled to the emergency lane of the interstate and put her head on her hands as they rested on the steering wheel.

"Oh, God, how am I ever going to get through this?" she cried.

Dumbfounded, Reese read the letter from Dan again. Divorce? Pam had filed for divorce? Then, picking up Pam's letter, fury blurred his eyes as he reread, *"I'm sorry I played along with Fiona and tricked you into marrying me. But now you'll have your freedom back. Freedom to marry Sharon, like she said you wanted to do. She said you two had always loved each other and that you'd be married now, if not for me."*

"SHARON!" Reese bellowed.

Sharon bolted into his office. "Yes?"

"You're fired!"

"Whaaat?" Disbelief clouded her well-made up face. "But, Reese, why?" She reverted to the little-girl voice he detested.

"Bainbridge Corporation no longer needs your services. You were mainly employed for Fiona's sake, and now that she's gone and I've finished my manuscript, you're just not needed anymore." He couldn't stand to even look at her while he talked. Because of her, he was losing Pam. Rage burned in his chest.

"Pack your bags. We're leaving for Dallas today."

"But Reese—"

"Just do it!" Reese yelled, flinging the letter on his desk and brushing past her.

As he left the room, Sharon carefully picked up the letter and read it. Reading the last words of the letter, she knew Pam had used her own words to destroy any chances she had of ever winning Reese. Dejectedly, she put the letter back on the desk and went to her room to pack.

For Pam, day four of her journey to nowhere started like the others. She started the Escalade and drove. She passed many tourist attractions, historical markers, and little out-of-the-way places that she knew under any other circumstances she would have loved to visit. But not in her present state of mind. All she could think about at this point was Reese.

She spent mile after endless mile just remembering their time together. She'd never dreamed she could love anyone as much as she loved Reese Bainbridge. In spite of his disagreeable moods, in spite of the things he accused her of, in spite of him believing only the worst of her, she still loved him. She loved the soft spot that she saw in him occasionally. She loved the tenderness he showed when they made love. Anyone who could be that tender and giving during lovemaking had to have a good heart, in spite of the outward façade he showed to the world.

And how could he make love to her like he had if he didn't care for her just a little? How—

How long had that State Patrol car been following her with its lights flashing? She pulled to the emergency lane and stopped. She let her window down and waited. What had she done wrong? Mentally, she went over any road rules she could have broken, and couldn't come up with anything.

"Ma'am, step out of the car, please," the state trooper directed.

Step out of the car? She was expecting him to ask for her driver's license, which she had already taken out of her purse and had in her hand.

"Ma'am! Step out of the car!"

Beginning to feel the slow rise of anger, Pam slowly got out of the Escalade.

"You have the right to remain silent—"

"WHAT? Right to remain silent? Are you arresting me for something?" Pam's indignant voice had risen, and now the other trooper, who had been standing beside the patrol car, made his way toward them.

"As a matter of fact, we are," the first trooper responded. "You're under arrest for auto theft. This car is reported stolen. You have the right—"

"Hold it one damn minute! This is my brother's vehicle. He loaned it to me for as long as I need it. You can call him and check for yourself!"

"Well, we'll do that when we get back to the station, but right now, if you'll stop interrupting me, I have to read you your rights. You have the right to remain silent—"

Pam sat silently in the back seat of the patrol car and fumed. What was going on? The big goon driving the car kept glancing in the rearview mirror at her as if he expected her to pull a gun and shoot him. She found it odd that they hadn't patted her down in search of a weapon. He'd told her his name was Jim as he helped her into the back seat. Like she gave a rat's ass what his name was. She just wanted to know what was going on.

The other trooper was following them in Tom's Escalade. This was just great! Tom was *not* going to believe she'd been arrested for stealing his SUV.

Soon they pulled into a police station in a small west Texas town. Once inside, Pam was led directly to a jail cell. "Don't I get a call?" she asked as the doors clanged shut in her face.

"You'll get your call soon enough," Jim answered, and walked away humming "The Yellow Rose of Texas."

Even more dazed than she was before, Pam sat numbly on the cot in the tiny jail cell and stared into space. She felt herself start to tremble with anger. Here she was, locked up in a jail in a small town in west Texas, where she knew no one, and she hadn't even been allowed to make a phone call. Was this possible? She could stay here for a very long time and no one would know where she was. She had called Tom every night, but they had both agreed that if she got busy with something, she might not call him. How many nights could pass before Tom got worried about her?

Feeling panic rising inside her, Pam leapt from the cot and grabbed the bars.

"HEY! SOMEBODY! I NEED SOME ANSWERS! I NEED TO MAKE A PHONE CALL! I DO HAVE A LAWYER, YOU KNOW!"

Nothing. Not a single sound from anywhere in the building. Had they locked her up and left? What if the building caught on fire? What if—

Okay, Pam, get a grip! Dully, she went back to the cot and sat down. She had to think of something, and if she panicked, she wouldn't be able to think at all. Making a concerted effort, she started to calm down.

"Okay, you can make your phone call now." Jim's voice brought Pam roughly awake. Had she actually lain down on that dinky little cot and gone to sleep? And for how long?

"What time is it?" she asked, glancing at her wristwatch. "Eight o'clock! How on earth did I sleep for that long?" she squeaked.

"I don't know, but the boys are sure glad you did. All that yelling was about to get on their nerves," Jim said, leading her to the front of the building. Was he trying to joke with her? He'd think "joke" when she finished slapping a lawsuit on him for wrongful arrest. She'd make him sorry—

"Okay, boys, here she is. I don't think she's suffered too much."

Pam stopped in her tracks. There in front of her stood Reese and Tom, with huge grins on their faces.

"Hey, little sis," Tom spoke first. "I hear you've been on a tear with the guys, here." He pulled her close in a big bear hug.

But even though Tom's arms felt better than almost anywhere else she could imagine being right now, Pam pulled away and scowled at him first, then Reese, who watched her intently with those amazing blue eyes.

159

"What's going on? Will someone please tell me what's going on?" Pam pleaded, still too weak from relief to allow her full ire to kick in.

"Well, it's like this," Tom started. "Reese came back to Dallas yesterday and found out you'd departed for parts unknown, and he kind of went berserk. He called his friend Jim Blalock, here, and told him to find you and arrest you for stealing my SUV. Then he and I jumped on the next flight out of Dallas and came after you. But I believe Reese needs to take the story from here. I might not get it right."

Pam slid her eyes to Reese. How she would love to go into his arms and tell him how much she loved him. The desire was so strong that she must have leaned in his direction, because before she knew what was happening, she *was* in his arms, his lips crashing down on hers, right there in front of everyone!

As breathtaking as it was, the kiss didn't last long. Reese stepped back from her, but kept his hands on her waist. "There are so many things I want to say to you, Pam, but not here with this hairy-legged audience. But I will ask you this, while I have witnesses. Will you marry me? I mean, again? This time I want to be sober and not stoned out of my head. I want to know that we're getting married for real." This brought a roar of laughter from the troopers standing around.

With tears flowing down her face, almost unable to believe that Reese Bainbridge had just proposed to her, Pam answered, "Yes! Yes! Yes!"

Again Reese pulled her to him and lowered his lips to hers, as the men standing around them cheered.

Everyone, that is, except Tom, who was too busy wiping the tears from his eyes.

Pam leaned back into the circle of Reese's protective arm. Was she dreaming? Were they really in a big limo, leaving the most beautiful wedding she had ever seen? *Her* wedding?

Almost having to pinch herself to make sure it was all real, Pam looked up into the loving eyes of Reese Bainbridge. His lips lowered to cover hers. She immediately responded to him. All it took was a look or a touch, and she was on fire for him.

"If we live together for fifty years, you'll continue to amaze me," he whispered against her lips. "When I thought I'd lost you, I realized that life without you wouldn't be living. I've never loved anyone like I love you, Pam. I've never even dreamed of loving anyone like I love you. Promise me that you'll never leave me again."

During the past few weeks of their engagement, while they planned the wedding, Reese had opened up to Pam. He had shared all of his desires, longings, and how badly he'd missed his parents as a child growing up. He told her how much he'd resented Fiona because he blamed her for driving his parents away from him.

"I promise, Reese. I won't ever intentionally hurt you. And I won't ever try to stop you from being the man that you are." If she could only make him know how much she loved him, Pam thought.

Reese sat forward and tapped on the glass that separated the driver from them. When the window slid open, he directed, "Drive to the cemetery."

At Pam's questioning look, he explained, "I want to say goodbye to Fiona. I didn't do a very good job of it the day we buried her."

When they reached the grave, Pam meant to wait in the car, but Reese took her hand and pulled her out with him. "I think she'd like to see us together, don't you?"

They walked hand in hand to Fiona's grave. Reese took the corsage from his lapel and, kneeling down, placed it on the grave. Pam knelt beside him. He kept her hand clutched in his.

"Fiona, I wanted to come by today and thank you for knowing me better than I knew myself. Thank you for bringing me the woman of my dreams. You old bat, you knew as soon as you saw Pam that I couldn't resist her, didn't you? You had already confiscated my stash of magazines!"

He stopped and wiped tears from his eyes, and from Pam's. But he soon continued, "Fifi, Pam and I got married today. I mean for real. Not some fast Vegas job that was done on the sly. We got married right here in Dallas, and all your snobby friends were at the wedding. We made you proud, old girl. I just wish you could have been here. I'm sorry for all the grief I caused you. I know now you mainly had my best interests in mind, but just didn't always know how to let me know that. Like I didn't always know how to let you know how I felt. Goodbye, Fifi, I love you."

As Reese stood and helped Pam to her feet, her attention was drawn to a flock of wild geese that flew overhead in a perfect V formation, honking and squawking their warnings that cold weather was on its way.

As she watched, the birds shifted and a new bird took the lead position. Pam was sure she heard Fiona's familiar cackle ring through the sky.

Epilogue

Pam put the finishing touches on the turkey and placed it in the oven. Reese put the tossed salad he'd been making into the refrigerator, and then opened his arms to Pam.

"Have you hugged your husband today, Mrs. Bainbridge?"

"Only about a hundred times," she answered, coming into his warm embrace.

"Well, do it again. I seem to have forgotten how wonderful it feels."

"Oh, my. He's already getting senile, and we haven't even been married a year yet," she spoke to the open room.

"I may get senile, but I'll never forget how to make love to you. That comes too naturally to forget."

"Is that a promise?" Pam asked, not able to comprehend the happiness she continued to experience.

"That's a promise," he assured her, claiming her lips in his.

"Reese, do you think they'll make it okay?" Pam asked, when she'd caught her breath.

"For the tenth time, they're going to be okay. We left the Jeep at the airport for them to come up the mountain in. Now relax and stop worrying. Everything's ready for their arrival, so come on over here and sit by the fireplace with me."

Pam sat snuggled against Reese and watched the fire sizzling and popping in the huge fireplace. Occasionally she glanced out the window at the gently falling snow. The peaks of the distant mountains were already white, and the ground outside the house was beginning to be covered, turning their home into a winter wonderland.

November. Thanksgiving. And the dreams she'd had of entertaining in this beautiful house were finally coming true. Tom and Jan were coming to South Carolina to spend the Thanksgiving weekend with them.

One of her biggest surprises had been Tom and Jan. It seemed they'd had a "thing" for each other since the first time Tom had come to the Winger & Thomas offices to see Pam, and had met Jan. She knew they liked to joke around with each other, but after Tom's accident, he'd stopped joking with Jan. Come to find out, he wasn't about to ask a woman to share his life if it was going to be spent in a wheelchair. But as soon as his back surgery was deemed a success and he was released from the doctor's care, he and Jan had started dating. They were going to be married in March.

They would live at Bainbridge Hall, with Reese and Pam's blessings, as Reese and Pam never wanted to live anywhere except here on the mountain. But Reese and Pam did go back to Dallas on a fairly regular basis because Reese had agreed, after much persuasion from Tom, to sit in on the board of directors of Bainbridge Corporation during their quarterly meetings.

"Pam?" Reese's voice brought her back to the present.

"Hmmm?" she mumbled, gazing into the fire.

"Do you see what I see?" he asked, pointing out the window.

Headlights of a vehicle were creeping slowly up the last incline of the mountain and approaching the house. Pam recognized Reese's Jeep.

Excitedly, she jumped up from the couch, pulling Reese with her, heading for the door.

Life just couldn't get any better than this. She was about to spend Thanksgiving with the people she loved the most. Just briefly, she wished Fiona could be here, but she soon forgot her glimpse of sadness as she welcomed her brother with open arms.

About the Author

Pat Ballard lives in Nashville, TN. She writes motivational romance novels with Big Beautiful Heroines to show that plus-size women can be just as sexy, romantic, and exciting as their slim sisters.

Visit Pat at www.patballard.com.

Check out other books by Pat—and more—at the Pearlsong Press website at www.pearlsong.com.

（